WINTERING

YEARLING BOOKS are designed especially to entertain and enlighten young people. Patricia Reilly Giff, consultant to this series, received her bachelor's degree from Marymount College and a master's degree in history from St. John's University. She holds a Professional Diploma in Reading and a Doctorate of Humane Letters from Hofstra University. She was a teacher and reading consultant for many years, and is the author of numerous books for young readers.

WINTERING

William Durbin

A YEARLING BOOK

Published by
Dell Yearling
an imprint of
Random House Children's Books
a division of Random House, Inc.
1540 Broadway
New York, New York 10036

Visit us on the Web! www.randomhouse.com/kids

Educators and librarians, for a variety of teaching tools, visit us at www.randomhouse.com/teachers

---

ISBN: 0-440-22759-3

Reprinted by arrangement with Delacorte Press

Printed in the United States of America

December 2000

10 9 8 7 6 5 4 3 2

OPM

To my daughter Jessica,
a student of history without equal

Foreword

Wintering continues the story of a young *voyageur* named Pierre La Page, begun in *The Broken Blade*. That first book is set in 1800 and follows Pierre on a twenty-four-hundred-mile canoe trip with a *voyageur* brigade from his home in Montréal to Grand Portage, on the western shore of Lake Superior, and back.

The *voyageurs* were travel-hardened canoemen who transported trade goods and furs along a four-thousand-mile waterway that extended from Montréal to the Pacific Ocean. They paddled fourteen to sixteen hours each day and carried loads of nearly two hundred pounds over many miles of rugged portages, stretches of land between lakes and rivers. Stopping for only two meals each day and sleeping under their overturned canoes at night, the *voyageurs* lived hard and often died young. Storytelling, singing, and smoking small clay pipes provided the men with their only relief from the backbreaking labor.

Wintering begins at Grand Portage in 1801, the year that saw the largest *rendezvous,* or meeting, in the history of the North West Company, Pierre's employer. Thanks to European fashion trends, the fur trade had become a multimillion-dollar industry. No well-dressed man went without a beaver hat, and no fine lady would be seen in public without a bit of fur trim on her coat or dress. With huge fortunes to be made, the Hudson's Bay Company and the newly formed XY Company were both pushing into territory controlled by the North West Company. In response, the North West called its partners together in the summer of 1801 to plan a strategy for maintaining its share of the trade.

Wintering traces Pierre's journey into the wilderness beyond Lake Superior during this dramatic year, and it follows him through his first winter in the north. In becoming an *hivernant,* or winterer, Pierre discovers much about himself and about the native people of the lake country, the Anishinaabe.

WILLIAM DURBIN
Lake Vermilion, Minnesota
April 1998

A Note of Special Thanks

I would like to thank my editor, Wendy Lamb, for her professional expertise, and my agent, Barbara Markowitz, for her friendship and her lifelong dedication to the world of books.

I'm also grateful to the staffs of the Minnesota Historical Society and the Hibbing Public Library, and to Gene Goodsky, Sherry Johnson, and Shelly Ceglar for their help with my research. And special thanks to my wife, Barbara, for her patience and support—I haven't forgotten that all the good ideas were yours.

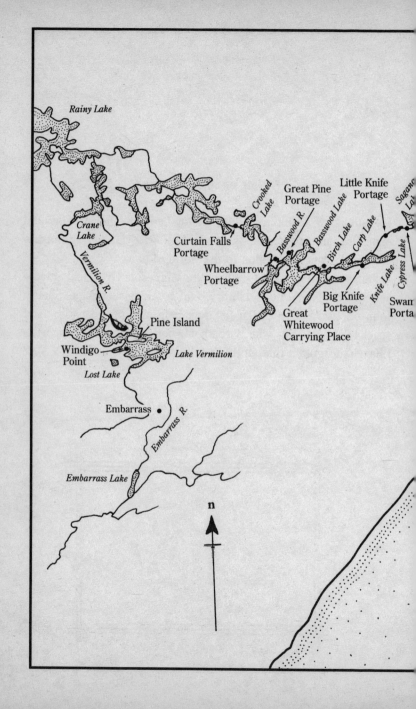

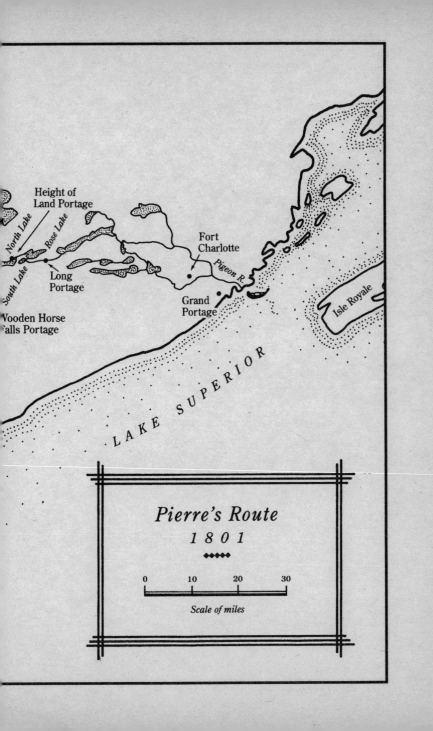

Height of
Land Portage

North Lake Rose Lake

South Lake

Long
Portage

Wooden Horse
Falls Portage

Fort
Charlotte

Pigeon R.

Grand
Portage

Isle Royale

LAKE SUPERIOR

Pierre's Route
1 8 0 1
◆◆◆◆◆

0   10   20   30

Scale of miles

CHAPTER 1

Bear for Breakfast

JULY 1801

"Breakfast off the port bow," Beloît called out.

Pierre La Page was half asleep, and the shout made him lurch forward. He rested his paddle blade on the gunwale of his canoe and looked up.

"Paddle, you fools," the bowman, Jean Beloît, yelled.

Suddenly the crewmen in all four canoes were pulling hard for the near shore.

Pierre was sick of paddling. The four-canoe brigade had started up the Pigeon River at four A.M., when the sun was only a faint glimmer in the pines, yet they still hadn't stopped for breakfast. This was Pierre's second summer with the North West Company, and though he was becoming a skilled canoeman, he was travel weary this morning. He had paddled and portaged more than twelve hundred miles since he'd left Montréal last May.

It was July now, and only two days ago his brigade had carried its trade goods over the legendary nine-mile trail at Grand Portage. He'd made four trips without complaint, carrying 180 pounds of goods up the trail and returning with an equal weight of bundled furs each time. It had nearly done him in. Pierre could understand why the old-timers joked that the North West Company used *voyageurs* to portage the freight because they couldn't risk laming mules or horses.

"I said paddle," Beloît yelled, pulling out his North West gun and aiming it over the bow.

Pierre squinted into the harsh light. Beloît was the grossest man Pierre had ever seen. Though most of the *voyageurs* took pride in their appearance, tying long fringed sashes around their waists and carefully perching their red woolen caps on their heads, Beloît was a picture of neglect. When he wasn't bare chested, his soiled shirt hung loosely over his hips. His sweat-stained cap often sagged down over his ears, and he refused to wear socks or deerskin leggings like the rest of the crew. Beloît's hair was long and greasy, and his perpetually bloodshot eyes were small and black. One of his front teeth was missing, and he always wore an evil grin made worse because the left half of his nose had been bitten off in a fight years ago, leaving only a ragged hole.

A moment later Beloît said, "Ship your oars." They

held their paddles still, and the canoes went into a silent glide.

When Pierre saw the bear, he felt sorry for it. Shooting an animal in the water wasn't sporting. Pierre's father always told him that the principle of fair chase meant all game should be given a chance. He said, "A true hunter, whether he's taking meat or seeking a trophy, honors his quarry by following the rules." The previous summer Pierre had watched his *voyageur* crew club a young doe to death while she was swimming across the Mattawa River, and the thought of it still bothered him.

Since the bear was only twenty yards from shore and swimming fast, Pierre thought it might escape. Then he heard the hammer click back on Beloît's gun. "Come on, sweet Tillie," Beloît whispered, talking to his gun as he always did just before he shot.

In the powder flash and roar that followed, a pair of mallards rose from a reed bed on the far shore. The crewmen cheered as the bear went limp in the water. Beloît shouted his favorite phrase, *"Je suis l'homme"* ("I am the man"), and waved his gun high overhead in a victory salute.

From his narrow seat in the middle of the canoe, Pierre stared at the bear. As it floated facedown in the water, blood pooled at its shoulder and paled to a misty pink, spreading outward into the clear waters of Mountain Lake. The bear smelled as bad as Pierre's dog, Pepper, did after he'd waded into a swamp.

"Roast bear for breakfast." Beloît grinned, showing his yellow teeth as he slipped a leather cord around the bear's foreleg and tied the loose end around his wrist. "Let's tow her to shore, *mesdemoiselles*."

The steersman in Pierre's canoe, a giant fellow whom the *voyageurs* called La Petite, cursed at Beloît and said, "Watch who you're calling girls, pretty boy," but Beloît only laughed harder.

When the canoe glided into the shallows, Beloît stepped out into the knee-deep water.

"You going to take a bath?" yelled the cook, André Bellegarde.

"Once a year is plenty," Beloît said, wrapping another turn of the cord around his wrist and bloodying his hands from the wound at the bear's shoulder. "Get your skinning knife ready, Bellegarde."

Then, as Beloît pulled the carcass toward shore, the bear lifted his head out of the water. With a horrifying sound that was part growl and part gurgling snort, the bear leaped up.

"No," Beloît hollered. Pulling hard on the leather cord, he tried to hold the bear back as it ran up the bank. "Noooo," he yelled a second time, planting his moccasins against a rock.

The crew stared openmouthed, as the line tightened and Beloît flew forward. He landed on his belly, and the bear dragged him toward the trees. Just when it looked as if the bowman was going to disappear into the woods, his head smacked into a huge red pine and the cord snapped.

Beloît lay flat on his stomach. He didn't even move when a pinecone fell from the tree and hit him squarely in the back. The crewmen stared silently. He's dead! Pierre thought.

When Beloît finally moaned and rolled over, all four canoes rocked with laughter.

His face was caked with mud and blood. The front of his shirt was covered with pine needles, a ragged hunk of moss stuck to his beard, and his dirty red cap was tilted to one side.

"You alive, Greenbeard?" Bellegarde chuckled.

Beloît, still dazed, grabbed the hunk of moss and dirt hanging on his chest. "Greenbeard, eh? Take this and flavor your soup."

As the clump of moss flew over Bellegarde's head and splashed into the lake, the crew had another good laugh.

Since it was already midmorning, the *voyageurs* moored their canoes in the shallows and stepped ashore for their usual breakfast—boiled corn and pork fat. Pierre was always amazed that the *voyageurs* could paddle twelve to sixteen hours a day on only two meals. They rose well before dawn and paddled until midmorning before they stopped for breakfast.

The mornings were hard on Pierre. At fourteen, he was always hungry. He'd added three inches and twenty pounds to his frame over the past winter, and he could never get enough to eat. He was already five feet, eight inches tall—taller than the average *voyageur*—and his canoe mates constantly teased him about his appetite and his size. They also joked about his blond hair and blue eyes, since nearly all the *voyageurs* were dark. "We'll have to get Blondie his own canoe if he grows any more," La Petite said as they climbed out of their canoes.

"No." The weasel-eyed cook paused to finger the white claw marks on the side of his face, left by a grizzly years earlier. "No. We'll just shorten his legs with my meat saw." Bellegarde roared at his fine joke.

Pierre didn't laugh. He missed his old canoe mate, Charles La Londe. La Londe had been a good-natured fellow who always walked with a bounce in his step. He was famous for his shoulder-length white hair, and no matter how dark or windy the day, he smiled and encouraged his fellow crewmen, unlike Bellegarde and Beloît, who lived to torture and tease. In Pierre's first days as a middleman last spring, his clumsy paddling had left his hands blistered and bloody. Yet La Londe had gone out of his way to teach him the proper rhythm and pace for an all-day paddle. "You've got to trick the work by dreaming of grander things," he had said.

Pierre often thought back to the terrible day when La Londe had drowned in the French River rapids. La Londe had saved his entire crew by jumping into the river and freeing the bow of their canoe from a rock, just as an oncoming canoe swept by. The only trace they found of his body was his cap and a single feather. Why did it have to be him? Pierre wondered.

As Bellegarde ladled a portion of corn onto Pierre's tin

plate, Pierre almost wished Beloît had killed the bear. He was starving.

Pierre knew that the men hated Beloît, but he thought someone would at least volunteer to inspect his wounds. However, they wolfed down their breakfast as if nothing unusual had happened. As soon as they sat back and lit their pipes, they began teasing him.

Bellegarde said, "I can't believe that weak-kneed scoundrel let two days of good meat run off into the woods without even putting up a struggle."

La Petite added, "No bear could best a real bowman," and the others joined in.

For once Beloît was speechless. Hoping for sympathy, he refused to wash his face or brush off his clothing, but the men were still teasing him after they'd packed away their tobacco pouches and boarded their canoes.

CHAPTER 2

The Rendezvous

The men pulled on their paddles, falling into the stroke-a-second pace they would hold all day. Portages and pipe stops provided the only break in their routine. The portages were always more work than paddling, so Pierre looked forward to the pipe stops every fifteen or twenty miles. Though Pierre didn't smoke, he enjoyed the rest. After the men moored their canoes at the water's edge, they would wade ashore and sit a few minutes in the shade of a tall pine, pulling on their little clay pipes and talking quietly.

The previous summer, during his first trip as a *voyageur,* Pierre had unwisely counted his paddle strokes early in the trip. After adding up an hour's paddling and multiplying it by the fifteen hours they'd paddled that day, Pierre found that he'd taken fifty-seven thousand strokes. Knowing the huge number made his job twice as hard. In fact, it was only after La Londe persuaded him to think of other things while he was paddling that his work became tolerable.

Pierre was still getting used to his north canoe. Only twenty-five feet long, it was trimmer than the big freight canoes his brigade had paddled from Montréal to Grand Portage this summer. Their craft carried the steersman, La Petite; the bowman, Beloît; Pierre; and three other middlemen, who sat amidships and did the bulk of the paddling.

Three thousand pounds of merchandise was stored between the seats of the canoe: kettles, ax heads, knives, guns, tobacco, cloth, ribbon, beads, and food, all packed in ninety-pound bales for portaging. They also carried two wooden kegs filled with gunpowder and sugar, and ten kegs of rum.

Pierre was excited about his first trip into the vast wilderness that lay north of Lake Superior. Once they turned off the main supply route and headed for their wintering post, they would be paddling through territory that had been seen by only a handful of white men. His father, Charles La Page, had been a North West steersman for most of his life, and he'd often told Pierre stories about the north. He had given Pierre some advice last May, the morning his brigade departed from his home in Lachine: "Never forget that you're a guest in the north," he said as Pierre hugged his mother one last time. "It's Anishinaabe country, and without their help, all our travel and trading would stop."

Pierre liked the sound of the word *Anishinaabe*. Though most people called the woodland tribes Ojibwe or Chippewa, Father knew the native language well enough to use the proper name. After his many winters trading in the north, he'd just been promoted to clerk of the North West Company depot in Lachine. He hated to give up his voyaging life, but Mother had talked him into accepting the position.

"Just think how nice it will be to rest from all that paddling," Mother said. "We'll keep each other company, and for once you can see one of your children grow up." She nodded toward Pierre's little sister, Claire, asleep under the feather-stuffed quilt in her cradle.

Just then La Petite started a song. *"En roulant ma boule, roulant,"* his big baritone voice boomed over the blue water. The *voyageurs* pulled hard on their paddles and waited to join in at the chorus. Singing made the days go faster, and men with good voices were rewarded with extra pay.

As Pierre paddled, his mind still reeled with images of last week's rendezvous back at Grand Portage. Pierre's brigade had arrived on July 1, 1801, just in time to see the largest gathering of North West Company officials in the history of the territory. Along with the Montréalers from back east and the wintering partners from the far north, three thousand *voyageurs* and Indians were present for the weeklong celebration.

After the long paddle from Montréal, the fort at Grand Portage was a welcome sight to Pierre. It was the largest and most famous fur depot in the Northwest Territory. A long wharf led to a gate and a palisade of vertical logs. Inside, the courtyard contained sixteen buildings, including the Great Hall, the cook shack, several warehouses and offices, and living quarters for company partners and clerks. The buildings were all made from hand-hewn timbers and cedar shingles, and except for their brown doors and windows, they were the same weathered gray as the outer walls of the stockade.

Every brigade stopped at Grand Portage for at least a brief *rendezvous,* or meeting. The crewmen celebrated, while the commanders met with company officials, tallied their suppliers, and planned the final details of their expeditions. The previous summer Pierre had paddled home to Montréal after the *rendezvous,* but this year he was headed north to spend the winter. There were only 150 miles and two dozen portages between him and the trading post where he would stay for the winter. The plan was to paddle from Grand Portage to Crane Lake. There his brigade would split into two groups. One party would travel north to Quetico Lake while the other headed south to Lake Vermilion. Each group would build a trading post, acquire furs, and return to Crane Lake with its pelts as soon as the lakes were free of ice the following spring.

Shortly after Pierre arrived at the fort, he was startled by a volley of gunshots and a deafening chorus of "Hurrah!" He sprinted over to La Petite. "What's going on?"

"Here comes the Premier," La Petite hollered over the raucous crowd of *voyageurs* and Ojibwe. Powder smoke drifted out across Portage Bay. Dogs barked up and down the shore.

"Who?" Pierre asked, squinting into the sun.

"Simon McTavish." La Petite leaned closer. "Premier is just his nickname. He's the head of the whole North West Company. Every official from here to Athabasca answers to him."

Father had often mentioned McTavish's name, but no one Pierre knew had ever seen him.

"He's come all the way from a big meeting in London," La Petite continued. "He's here to rally us for a big push this season. They say heads will roll if that new XY Company takes over any more of our trade routes."

"I thought our only competition was the Hudson's Bay?" Pierre asked.

"It's the combination," La Petite said. "With the XY men and the international border dispute working against us down here, and Hudson's Bay men pushing down from the north, they're afraid we might get squeezed out. Our company's stock is worth half of what it was five years ago." La Petite still had his eyes on the pier. "Look! Here he comes!"

The cheers were even louder now. Four men hoisted McTavish onto their shoulders and carried him through the gates of the fort. "McTavish loves a show," La Petite said. "That's how he always comes ashore."

The next morning another famous Norwester, John

McDonald, a towering Scotsman, marched through the fort gates with a long sword buckled at his waist. Pierre heard a fellow leaning against the east palisade whisper, "You'll not find a more dangerous man on this earth. He'd sooner run you through with his sword than look at you."

As he studied the bold characters arriving for the *rendezvous,* Pierre was disappointed in his own commander, William McHenry. Tall and pale, McHenry wore a blue waistcoast, a flat-topped hat, and a look of perpetual confusion. On the trip from Montréal he'd spent most of his evenings alone in his tent, reading his books or writing in his journal. McHenry left the daily management of the crew to La Petite or Maurice Blondeau, the most experienced *voyageurs*.

Soon after he arrived at Grand Portage, Pierre decided to walk to the Ojibwe camp and visit Mukwa, the local chief. The previous summer Pierre's friend Jacques Charbonneau had introduced him to Mukwa and his family. Though Mukwa was a colorful fellow, Pierre was mainly interested in seeing his dark-eyed daughter, Kennewah. A year had passed since he had last visited this village, yet the picture of her shy smile, her shining black hair, and her soft doeskin dress was as clear in Pierre's mind as if he had seen her yesterday.

When Pierre told La Petite he was going up to the village, Beloît overheard. "So is little La Page going to see his *mademoiselle*?" Beloît's black eyes glittered as he wiped his scarred nose with a dirty hand. "What was her name again? Many Kisses?"

When Pierre blushed, Beloît laughed.

"Her name is Kennewah," Pierre said, hurrying up the trail. How he hated Beloît!

"That's just what I said," Beloît hollered after him, "Kennewah Many Kisses." He roared so loudly that Pierre was sure every man in Grand Portage heard his cackle.

Pierre hurried along the river path that divided the *voyageurs* into two camps—the pork eaters and the *hivernants*. The pork eaters were men who paddled from Montréal to Grand Portage and never ventured further north. They slept under their canoes just as they did on the trail. The *hivernants* were men who wintered in the north. They looked with disdain on the pork eaters and were privileged to lodge in tents. Fights were common between the two groups. Pierre would remain a pork eater until he hiked over the Grand Portage and paddled as far as the Height of the Land, the point where the rivers began flowing north.

Just beyond the *voyageur* encampment lay the canoe works. It was here that Pierre had first met Mukwa, who dressed outrageously in bright shirts and waistcoats and ostrich feathers but treated his friends with courtesy.

The Ojibwe band built about seventy canoes annually for the North West Company, and along the shore, boats stood in various stages of completion. Pierre approached two men who were painting the gunwales of a north canoe in alternate swatches of green, red, and white. "Where can I find Mukwa?" he asked.

They both shook their heads and said, *"Nibowin."* Pierre tried "Kennewah," but they repeated, *"Nibowin."*

Did *nibowin* mean they didn't know French? Pierre walked up to the village. He found Mukwa's wigwam, but no one was home. After waiting all winter to see Kennewah again, he would have to wait yet another day.

Though he and Kennewah had spent only a short time together, she'd become as special to him as his friend Celeste back in Lachine. Celeste was the daughter of a wealthy doctor, and she and Pierre attended the same school. She was the only person he'd ever confided in about his dream of attending college someday. When Pierre reenrolled as a *voyageur* in the spring, they'd even joked about getting married.

Pierre would never forget the moment. He and Celeste were walking along the bank of the St. Lawrence, enjoying the first real warmth of the season. An early brigade was readying for departure, and just ahead, four men were carrying a thirty-five-foot Montréal canoe toward the water.

"If I was Madame La Page," Celeste teased, "could I ride with you in your canoe?"

"Why, of course, *mademoiselle,*" he laughed. "I would throw a parcel of trade goods into the river and make a special seat just for you."

"How gallant of you, *monsieur.*" Celeste offered Pierre her hand and curtsied.

"For Your Ladyship, nothing would be too good." Pierre continued the game by bowing low and kissing the back of her wrist. "And each night I would save you the sweetest piece of pork fat from my corn soup."

When he looked up, Celeste wrinkled her nose. "Pork fat? We mustn't become too familiar, Monsieur La Page." Her blue eyes danced mischievously as she pulled back her hand and tossed her white shawl over her shoulder. Her fine black hair, which was normally gathered into a tight braid, hung loosely down her back that day.

Though the joking was fun, it made him feel sad. Since he was only fourteen, and his family were paupers compared to the Guilliards, he knew that no matter how much he and Celeste liked each other, their talk of marriage must remain a joke. Unless, by some miracle, he could earn enough money to complete his education and raise his station in life, there was no hope for him to marry Celeste.

So his trip this summer was tied to a twofold dream. But his feelings for Kennewah complicated the picture. He'd never said a word to Celeste about her. Even though Kennewah had written Pierre a letter at Christmas—she was improving her French with the help of a Catholic missionary—and had sent it to Lachine with a *voyageur,* Pierre never mentioned it. If Kennewah was just a friend, Pierre should have been honest and told Celeste. He could have said, "Did I tell you about the nice Ojibwe girl I met at Grand Portage?"

It should have been so easy, but it wasn't. And now that Pierre was about to meet Kennewah again, he could admit the reason for his hesitancy. He would never be sure of his feelings for Celeste until he spoke with Kennewah one more time.

When he returned to the *voyageur* camp, La Petite approached Pierre. He kept his voice low and winked. "How was Kennewah?"

"I couldn't find her," Pierre said. "I asked two fellows about her, but they couldn't speak French. They kept saying *nibowin*."

La Petite shrugged. "We'll be here the rest of the week; you'll have plenty of time to—"

"Did you say *nibowin*?" Bellegarde interrupted.

Pierre nodded.

Fingering his scarred cheek, Bellegarde said, "That's too bad, son."

"What do you mean?"

"*Nibowin* means dead."

"It can't!" Pierre cried. There was so much he needed to say to Kennewah.

"Damn," La Petite said. "I was afraid of that. The men were saying that smallpox hit hard up here last winter. Some of the villages lost half their people."

"*Nibowin?*" Pierre repeated. He thought of Kennewah's dark eyes and ebony hair . . . her innocence . . . her gentle humor . . .

Bellegarde nodded. "I'm sorry, son. It's hard, but lots of these Indians live short lives."

La Petite patted Pierre on the shoulder. "The deck's

stacked against them. If smallpox doesn't do 'em in, consumption, diphtheria, and syphilis are waiting their turn. They've got no way to fight the white man's diseases."

Pierre walked back to the Ojibwe village, hoping to find that he had misunderstood. Bellegarde came along to interpret. They soon found a nephew of Mukwa's, who confirmed that the worst had happened.

"The only member of Mukwa's family to survive the epidemic was the old grandmother," the nephew explained through Bellegarde. "And after she prepared the last body for burial—it was her little grandson Kewatin—and helped carry him to the grave house, she cut off all her hair and walked off into the woods to die."

His words sounded cold and matter-of-fact. When so many died, Pierre supposed, funerals became commonplace.

As the nephew finished speaking, he touched the bear claw necklace around Bellegarde's neck and pointed to the scars on the cook's face. Bellegarde smiled. He was proud of surviving a grizzly bear attack, and he loved to tell the story.

"We was in the foothills of the Rockies . . . ," Bellegarde began.

Pierre walked away; he needed to be alone. Without any clear destination in mind, he wandered toward Mount Rose, a rocky hill that overlooked the fort. What would he have said to Kennewah? He'd imagined the meeting a hundred times during his long paddle from

Montréal, but he'd never got beyond a simple hello. Did it matter now?

The trail wound back and forth across the south face of the ridge. In places huge piles of slate had fallen off the cliff, and on the steepest part of the trail, little steps had been chipped out of the rock for footholds. When Pierre reached the summit his heart was pounding.

He looked out over Portage Bay and past Hat Point to the great lake beyond. To the south was the hillside where he and Kennewah had picked blueberries the previous summer. They'd met by accident. She was so beautiful that Pierre had been afraid to breathe. In his nervousness he'd tipped over a berry basket, but Kennewah had only laughed. Pierre was used to the jeers of the school yard and the evil cackling of Beloît, but her laughter was without ridicule or scorn. That was when Pierre smiled, too.

Though Kennewah knew only a little French and he knew even less Ojibwe, they spent the whole afternoon together, filling her birch berry baskets and hiking and laughing. . . .

Laughing, Pierre thought. That was only a summer ago, yet she would never laugh again.

He looked inland. A slight dip in the tree line revealed the famous Grand Portage gap and the trail that would soon take him deep into the wilderness.

He turned to stare at the miniature men and buildings below. The sun was sinking fast. For the moment it was easy to pretend he was a god, enthroned on a stone mountain, sitting in silent judgment of the world. Though the Great Hall was barely a stone's throw away, in the pink and purple haze it looked as if it were many miles distant.

If only, Pierre thought, I could point a finger and right the wrongs of this world. If only fools like Beloît could be sent to the eternal damnation they deserve and bright souls like Kennewah and Mukwa and La Londe could live to light the world.

Pierre wished he could sit on the mountain all night. It would be dark and quiet soon—a perfect place to be alone and think. He didn't feel like talking to anyone right now, and he knew that the *voyageurs* would celebrate tonight. He could already hear a fiddle and a flute tuning up for their dance.

Once the fur presses closed down for the day, the two busiest places in Grand Portage were the canteen and the jail. As hard as the *voyageurs* worked, they played even harder. The *hivernants* got especially rowdy at night—La Petite said they were "woods queer" from all those months alone in the wilderness—and at least a dozen were thrown into the stockade every day. It wasn't unusual for a man to squander a month's wages on liquor in a single night. "And the more they spend," La Petite said, "the more likely it is they'll buy themselves a night's lodging in the guardhouse."

While the canoemen celebrated outside the palisades, the company officials held fancy balls inside the fort. According to Commander McHenry, the Great Hall blazed with dozens of candles, and the Norwesters celebrated till dawn. Dressed in their best Eastern finery, the company partners and their guests danced highland flings, quadrilles, reels, and square dances accompanied by violins and bagpipes. Between dances they drank wine and feasted on trout, smoked whitefish, venison, buffalo tongue, beaver tail, and fresh butter.

In the *voyageur* camps a squeaky fiddle and a sailor's pipe played, while the canoemen danced and sang and told stories through the night. And the background noise of drums, howling dogs, shrieks, and gunshots never distracted them for a moment.

Pierre rubbed his brow at the thought of an all-night party. What he needed now was quiet. How could he sort through his feelings, surrounded by two thousand crazy French-Canadians who were drinking themselves into oblivion?

Why, in a world of violent, crazy men, should someone as gentle as Kennewah have to be the one to die?

CHAPTER 3

The Long Carry

When Pierre got back to the fort, the *voyageurs* were all talking about a carry, or portage, that a man in Daniel Harmon's brigade had completed that very afternoon. According to the men, the fellow Norwester had brought two ninety-pound parcels of trade goods to Fort Charlotte and returned with two packs of furs in only four hours.

Beloît declared, "I can't see why anyone would make a fuss over a simple day's work!"

Harmon's men were camped next to McHenry's crew, and they fell silent. Finally a dark man stood up. "Are you claiming you could do as well, Jean Beloît?"

"Je suis l'homme!" Beloît said, and Harmon's crew laughed at his boldness. "If I was inclined to bust a gut, I

22

don't doubt I could match any of you sissies. But I know a fellow who could double that carry."

"And who might that be?"

Pierre watched La Petite glare at Beloît, but there was no stopping him now. "I'm talking, of course, about my good friend here," Beloît continued, "Monsieur Petite."

"Joseph Jourdain, you say?" the man replied. A murmur rose from his crewmates. Everyone knew La Petite's reputation.

In a moment the odds were set. It was three to one against La Petite carrying a 360-pound load to Fort Charlotte and back in four hours. To pacify his friend, Beloît declared that twenty Spanish dollars would go to La Petite if he achieved the carry. But even with such a prize, La Petite wagged a finger in Beloît's face, saying, "If you ever enter me in a contest again without asking, I'll feed you to the trout."

The event began at six the following morning. "Work is not so bad if it is finished before the heat of the day," La Petite declared as McHenry and Harmon compared their watches. The entire population of Grand Portage was on hand to watch. Beloît and Bellegarde helped La Petite strap three packs across his back and one in front of his chest. The crowd cheered as La Petite started up the trail.

Pierre worried about LaPetite, for lifting too much could ruin a man. The doctors called it "strangulated hernia," but to Pierre's father it was simply "ripping your guts out." Pierre's uncle had died that way at only twenty-three, and according to his father, hernias killed more *voyageurs* than all the white water and Indians in the Northwest Territory.

Like all long carries, this one was divided into *poses,* or short rests. Several dozen people followed La Petite to the first *pose,* but only a handful of men trailed on from there.

At first it looked as if La Petite would make the carry with ease, resting only briefly at the second and third *poses.* But as the hill got steeper, his steps shortened, and his breath got quick and shallow.

Sweat soon beaded his forehead, and he was wheezing like an exhausted runner. "You can do it," Pierre called.

At the next *pose,* La Petite collapsed with his pack straps in place, and the awkward load tipped him over onto his side.

Beloît got down on all fours and stuck his nose in La Petite's face. "We're nearly to the flat," he declared. "The tough part's done." Pierre felt like yelling, "Leave him alone!" but La Petite took up his load again.

When Fort Charlotte was still an hour away, Pierre suddenly realized that the big man would make it. In that instant Pierre saw that the secret of a great carry was the same as the secret of an all-day paddle.

He recalled some advice that La Londe had offered the previous summer. At the time he didn't understand it, but today it made sense. "A tough portage or a hard paddle is the same," La Londe said. "You must give yourself over to the power of the hill, just as a paddler must lose himself in the rhythm of the waves."

When La Petite arrived back at Grand Portage with four parcels of furs, cheers sounded throughout the fort. Pierre knew he'd witnessed an event that would outlive them all. Even before the packs were lifted from La Petite's shoulders, the money was changing hands.

Beloît was counting coins like a greedy child when La Petite suddenly called, "Beloît." For a moment Pierre thought La Petite had injured himself. "Jean Beloît," La Petite repeated, "we are not yet done."

The silent crowd watched as Beloît walked over and stood before him. "Turn around," La Petite commanded.

Then La Petite lifted a dusty pack from the ground and hooked it over Beloît's shoulders. He did the same with a second pack. Beloît was silent until La Petite reached for another.

"No," Beloît croaked as the third pack was hooked in front of his chest, and he tipped forward. The veins on his temples popped out, and his legs trembled. Everyone was grinning at what would happen next.

When the full weight of the last pack hit him, Beloît's legs gave out. The crowd roared as he flew backward, his eyes wide and his hands clutching at air.

Only then did La Petite declare, "Now we are done, Brother Jean."

From that day forward things happened fast. Half of the crew who'd arrived with Pierre paddled home to Montréal with bundled furs, while McHenry gathered together the small group he was taking north. They would be traveling in a four-canoe brigade as far as Crane Lake. From there, two canoes would paddle north to establish a winter trading post on Quetico Lake, while the other two headed south to do the same on Lake Vermilion.

Along with the men Pierre already knew—La Petite, Bellegarde, and Beloît—the commander added two new recruits to his canoe: a young *voyageur* named Amblé Le Clair, who, like Pierre, would be spending his first winter in the north; and an older fellow, Augustine Delacroix.

Amblé's nickname was Louie, after his middle name, Louis; but since he had a high, squeaky voice and tended to talk a lot, the men called him Squeaks, Noise Box, Squirrel, or Ramble. Louie laughed off the teasing, and the men soon discovered that if they teased him too much, he got so excited that he talked even more.

The men called Augustine by his full name at all times. Short, thick-chested, and bald, he was very old for a *voyageur*—Pierre guessed he was over fifty—and he kept to himself. One day Pierre asked him how long he'd been a *voyageur*.

"A *voyageur* I'm not," Augustine spat. "For forty years I've been a sailor. I've seen every port from Singapore to Cape Horn." He jerked his head toward Lake Superior. "No man can voyage on a pond such as this."

As he strode away, La Petite chuckled. "You'll have to excuse him, Pierre. After all those years at sea, he finally decided to settle down on a small farm outside Montréal. But when he came home last spring, his wife had run off with the local butcher. He enrolled with the North West Company the very next day."

"And he's going to winter over?" Pierre asked.

La Petite nodded. "He wants to get as far away from that woman as he possibly can."

Pierre hoped the old fellow's mood would improve. He couldn't imagine wintering with two ill-tempered characters like Beloît and Augustine.

CHAPTER 4

Height of the Land

"Be careful, schoolboy," Beloît said. "That pack weighs a whole lot more than a spelling book."

For a moment the words didn't mean much to Pierre. He'd been thinking about Kennewah. Ever since he had learned she was dead, he could think of little else. Even his hike two days earlier across the Grand Portage—the famous carry he'd been waiting a year to complete—had only been a blur. Four times he'd carried his required two packs of trade goods up the trail to Fort Charlotte and returned with two bundles of furs, but his heart wasn't in it.

That day the nine-mile portage had been a dream world, peopled by faces of the dead. Once he saw Mukwa standing in the ostrich-plumed hat he loved to wear. The chief looked so real that Pierre had to rub his eyes and blink away the image. Another time Pierre pictured a feast in Mukwa's wigwam. Kennewah held her baby brother, Kewatin, on her lap, and as the little boy nibbled on some maple candy, he pointed his tiny finger at Pierre and grinned.

"Do you hear me, schoolboy? That's no spelling book." Beloît shocked Pierre back to reality.

"At least I know how to spell more than *rum* and *tavern*," Pierre snapped back. Pierre had learned that Beloît respected people who stood up to him. But when Beloît eyed a nearby pistol, Pierre thought he'd gone too far.

Beloît looked sideways at Pierre with his black eyes shining. Pierre held his breath until Beloît slapped his knee. "If they'd learned me to spell fine words like *tavern*, in school," he said with a laugh, "I might've stayed past the third grade."

"You dropped out in third grade?" Pierre asked, struggling to imagine him as a little boy in knee breeches.

"You heard right." Beloît laughed again. "They were so cheap, they kept that school awful cold. One day the sister told me I'd burn in hellfire if I kept using the Lord's name in vain. So I stood up and said, 'At least I'll be warm there,' and I walked right out the door."

"Stop filling the boy's head with nonsense," La Petite said. "We've got important things to do this afternoon."

"Such as?" Beloît countered.

"Such as baptisms." La Petite winked.

Pierre frowned. What did they mean? He was still tired from the two-thousand-yard Rose Lake portage. Augustine had cursed it as "a path unfit for goats." The old sailor was especially angry because it was his turn to carry one of McHenry's book crates. The commander had two heavy wooden crates filled with books, and they caused a lot of grumbling among the men.

"What do you suppose they mean by baptisms?" Louie asked Pierre.

"Caulk that mouth, Noise Box," Beloît sneered. "We got big plans."

When Louie asked, "What sort of plans?" Beloît tossed him a pack. "Cork it, Squeaks. Plans that will never happen if you don't stop flappin' your lips and start portaging."

McHenry patted Louie on the shoulder and said, "Remember, lad, 'In silence there is a worth that brings no risk.' "

Pierre grinned. This quote from Plutarch was one of his teacher Sister André's favorites. Louie reminded him of a cousin back in Lachine who always got in trouble because he couldn't keep his mouth shut. Pierre had talked with Louie quite a bit during the first part of their trip, but Louie didn't like to discuss his past. The only thing Pierre knew for sure was that Louie's father had traveled to Paris on a business trip the previous year, and for some reason he had never returned. Louie's mother and his three little sisters had moved in with his grandparents, but the house was so crowded that Louie thought it best to sign on as a *voyageur*. "Sleeping under a canoe is a lot less crowded than our little house was," he said, "and a lot quieter, too."

"Quieter than spending all day and all night with Beloît?" Pierre asked.

"Without a doubt," Louie said, smiling. Pierre wondered just how difficult Louie's former life had been.

After the brigade crossed South Lake, they reached the Height of the Land portage. Pierre's father often told him about this famous continental divide. Here, rivers to the north flowed all the way to Hudson's Bay, while the waters to the south ran through the Great Lakes and eventually reached the Atlantic Ocean.

The minute they finished their last carry, La Petite called Pierre and Louie to his side. "Gentlemen," he began, "as newcomers entering the waters of the Northwest Territory for the very first time, it is my honor to accept you into a rare corps of men."

Commander McHenry, who was standing off to one side, grinned as La Petite began his speech. At the same time, a dozen men appeared behind La Petite, carrying their muskets.

"Are you ready, Bellegarde?" La Petite asked, and the greasy cook stepped forward, toting a copper kettle filled with lake water. In his free hand he held a cedar bough.

La Petite winked at the *voyageurs*, who were now crowded close around him. "Let's get this ceremony started." He turned to Pierre and Louie and said, "Repeat after me."

Pierre, blushing at all the attention, repeated, "I, Pierre Charles La Page . . . do solemnly promise to never let a new hand pass into the waters of the northwest . . . without first administering this same ceremony which I now attend."

As he and Louie recited their lines, the men on all sides nodded.

"And furthermore," Pierre repeated, blushing brighter, "I swear that I will never kiss a *voyageur*'s wife without her permission."

At this point Bellegarde shouted, "You keep your lips off my Rosie, La Page, permission or not, or I'll skin your hide." At the thought of Pierre romancing Bellegarde's old, toothless wife, the men roared with laughter.

After the laughter died down, La Petite asked Pierre and Louie to kneel. Then he dipped the cedar bough in the kettle and sprinkled each boy with a few drops of lake water. "I now declare you *hommes du nord*—men of the north," he said.

The men cheered and threw their hats into the air, as twelve North West guns fired one after another. Before the powder smoke had cleared, Bellegarde appeared with a keg under his arm and a tin cup in his hand.

The whole brigade lined up at the keg, and as soon as their cups were all filled, McHenry raised his hand to quiet the rowdy men. "Before we all celebrate—and knowing the likes of you, I'm sure it's celebrating that you have on your minds—we must toast these former boys, who now stand before us as men." He paused to raise his battered tin cup in a salute and said, "To Monsieur Pierre La Page and Monsieur Amblé Le Clair—north men for now and ever after."

Though Louie immediately raised his cup to take a swig, Pierre hesitated. He recalled the previous summer, when in his haste to prove himself a man, he'd drunk several glasses of rum. It had given him a headache he would never forget. He smiled and swallowed one small taste, trying not to choke on the burning liquid.

Most of the men downed their drams in a single gulp and crowded around Bellegarde for a second shot. Though Bellegarde offered Pierre a refill, he shook his head.

Pierre knew the *voyageurs* usually didn't begin celebrating till after supper was served and the campfire was blazing high. So it was strange to watch the men celebrate so frantically in daylight. But this was true to the character of the canoemen. If there was food, they ate till it was gone; if there was rum, they drank till they emptied the kegs. *Voyageurs* did nothing in moderation. Quick to anger and just as quick to forgive, they lived hard and died young. Only last June Pierre had watched La Petite and Beloît beat each other senseless during supper, then forget their argument before bedtime.

By late afternoon the singing and storytelling were at a fever pitch. Pierre set his full cup down on a log and studied McHenry. Though the commander had taken off his coat in the heat of the day, he still wore his tall, wide-brimmed felt hat.

McHenry was sitting beside Maurice Blondeau and listening to Beloît tell a story, or more likely a lie. McHenry looked like a pale preacher who should be riding off on a nag to deliver a sermon at a country church.

When McHenry retired to his tent a short while later, Pierre turned to La Petite. "The commander sure doesn't look like he's spent much time in the north," Pierre began.

"McHenry?" La Petite looked surprised. "Why, he's traveled more miles in the wilderness than any two of us added together! He's only with the North West because he quit the Hudson's Bay Company. He was one of the first white men to cross the Arctic Barrens. He commanded the expedition that—" La Petite stopped suddenly when a cheer rose from the other side of the fire. "Looks like a little contest. Let's see if it's worth a wager."

Pierre trailed behind, thinking. McHenry a famous Arctic explorer? Surely not.

He wanted to ask more questions, but La Petite had other things on his mind. The men were getting ready for a knife-throwing contest.

"The first to hit the mark wins the pot," Beloît explained as he pulled a half-burned stick from the fire and drew an X on a fat birch tree. "Place your bets in the hat here." Pierre looked down at Beloît's greasy red cap. He remembered last summer when Beloît couldn't find a plate and ate his supper right out of that cap. It looked as if it hadn't been washed since then.

La Petite and Pierre each tossed in a coin. "We start at ten paces," Beloît said, counting his steps as he walked away from the stump. He scratched a line in the forest duff with the heel of his moccasin. The damp odor of the soil beneath the pine needles reminded Pierre of how his mother's flower garden smelled in early spring. Though Father teased her about "wasting good garden space on things a man can't eat," Pierre knew he was proud when the neighbors commented on how colorful and bright their front yard looked.

Each man took a turn with his knife. Some were experienced throwers who balanced the bright steel lightly across their fingers and tossed with a quick flick of the wrist. Others were amateurs who swung their whole arms and hit the tree with the flat side of their blades as often as they buried the point. One man even missed the tree altogether. And when Louie buried his knife handle first in the ground at the base of the tree, Beloît hollered, "Gads, Squeaks. Didn't your mama ever teach you back from front?"

Louie hung his head. "You'll hit her next time," Pierre said, clapping him on the shoulder.

But the most frightening toss of all was made by a drunken man named Balanger. When he drew back to throw, his knife slipped out of his hand and spun straight into the air. Everyone dove for the bushes. After the knife clattered off the hull of a canoe, Beloît leaped up and took a coin from his cap. "Here's your money," he said, pressing it into Balanger's hand. "You take a seat now and let the rest of us have a try."

When Pierre took his turn, the men whistled as he drew out his finely honed blade. "There's a real knife for you," La Petite said.

As the hand-tempered steel glistened in the firelight, Pierre thought of Charles La Londe, who had given the knife to him just before he drowned.

Pierre's throw missed the mark by a foot, but his blade buried deep in the white bark, and the men gave a little cheer. Pierre was not very experienced with a knife. Though his mother allowed him to whittle with his jack-knife back home, she took it away whenever she caught him playing mumblety-peg or tossing it at a tree or a fence post. He and a schoolmate sometimes practiced throwing their knives behind the barn, but more often than not, Mother found them out.

The man who most impressed Pierre with his knife throwing was the old sailor, Augustine. Though only two men got closer to the target than Pierre, Augustine's very first throw hit just an inch below the X. The more Pierre got to know Augustine, the more he admired him. Though he had huge, powerful hands and arms that gave him a rugged look, he took great pride in his appearance. Unlike most of the men, who bathed only on Sunday afternoons, Augustine washed in the lake each evening, and every morning he carefully shaved his bald head and face with his hunting knife. He kept his blade so sharp that no one but Beloît ever dared tease him.

Sensing that Augustine might win in the next round, Beloît said, "Not bad for an old sea dog, Auggie."

"My name is Augustine." He clenched his fist tight. As the muscles in his forearm flexed, the blue outline of a tattooed palm tree swayed back and forth.

"All right, Auggie," Beloît said.

Pierre couldn't believe Beloît's nerve. Augustine's eyes narrowed in rage, and he took a step forward. But just before he got within swinging distance, Beloît laughed, "Just kidding, old mate." Then he slapped Augustine's shoulder.

"It ain't mate," Augustine said, stiffening, "and it ain't Auggie. And don't you ever forget it."

"All right, sailor, whatever you say." Beloît smiled, turning to the rest of the men. "Let's get on with it, boys."

Beloît's tactic worked; Augustine was so angry that on his next try he nearly missed the tree.

"Too bad, old salt," Beloît crowed, "maybe you'll have an easier time at eight paces." Beloît measured the distance with his eye and drew his knife back. He missed, and so did everyone else.

When Augustine's turn came, he stepped up and threw before Beloît had a chance to needle him. His blade flashed through the air and hit the *X* with a loud *thunk*. Everyone clapped the old sailor on the back. "Well thrown, *monsieur*," La Petite said.

"We'll see about that," Beloît mumbled, walking forward to examine the target. He pulled Augustine's blade out and tossed it to the ground. "You never touched the mark."

"What kind of rubbish is that?" Augustine shouted, trotting toward the birch.

"Look for yourself! We'll just have to divide these bets back up." Beloît reached for his coin-filled cap.

"Hands off!" Augustine hollered. He picked up his knife and whirled toward Beloît.

"No!" Pierre shouted as Augustine's blade flashed in the air.

Pierre blinked. The knife grazed the back of Beloît's wrist and pinned his cap to the log. Beloît lifted his hand and stared at the bright channel of blood.

With a sick grin, Beloît reached down and pulled the knife from the log. As he stepped toward Augustine, he picked up his cap with his left hand. It was so quiet that Pierre could hear the rustling of a bird at the edge of the woods.

When Beloît reached Augustine, he pointed the knife directly into his stomach, saying, "Now that's what I call a fine throw, Auggie." Then he flipped the knife toward him and handed him the capful of coins. "Here's your winnings."

Augustine caught his knife by the handle and resheathed it. He poured the coins into his hand and gave the cap back. "I earned the francs, but I don't want your damn dirty cap," he said, grinning.

Beloît grinned then, too, and poking his finger through

the knife hole, said, "A little extra ventilation won't hurt this old bonnet." He put his greasy cap back on his head, and the whole camp had a good laugh.

A few minutes later Augustine pulled out a little sailor's pipe and played a lively jig. "Dance time," Beloît called. He wiped his bleeding wrist on his shirt front and led the men in a wild dance.

As the crazy bowman jigged his way around the rock-ringed campfire, Pierre could see the last light of the setting sun shining through the slit in Beloît's cap. Pierre was glad the men had declared a truce. How sad and stupid it would be to bury a man because of a senseless quarrel and leave a broken paddle blade to mark a grave on this lonely shore.

CHAPTER 5

Saganaga

"Daylight in the swamp, mesdemoiselles!" Beloît yelled as he beat on the side of Bellegarde's kettle with a spoon.

Pierre woke out of a sound sleep. Throwing off his blanket, he sat up and bumped his head on the ash thwart of the canoe.

It was four A.M., the usual time for departure, but after their long night of celebrating the men were still snoring.

When Beloît saw that the kettle had little effect, he got out his North West gun. He winked at Pierre. "Tillie will wake these laggards from their dreams," he said, pouring a measure of powder down the barrel and ramming a patch home. He didn't bother to waste a ball.

Pierre blinked his sleep-swollen eyes as Beloît drew back the hammer of his gun and pointed it skyward.

Pierre couldn't believe that any man could be so mean. Pierre shook his head, hoping he would stop, but Beloît only grinned.

The whole world exploded when he touched the trigger. Men on all sides leaped up and ran for their rifles. Bellegarde yelled, "Indians!" Louie tripped and fell into the ashes of the fire.

When the men realized what had happened, sticks, stones, and curses flew at Beloît. He just laughed.

After they had boarded their canoes and started up North Lake, McHenry tried to soothe their raw nerves. "It's all downstream from here, gentlemen," he announced. Pierre looked into the still water. The commander must be joking. Though the map might say they'd reached the point where the waters flowed north, there wasn't any noticeable current yet.

Beloît was his usual cackling self, while the rest of the crew were silent and glum, with yellowish complexions and black circles under their eyes.

Pierre was amazed at how quickly the men recovered. By the midmorning breakfast stop, Beloît and Augustine were joking together. "That sure was a fine party last night, eh, Beloît?" Augustine said as he wolfed down huge mouthfuls of boiled corn. "I ain't had such a fine time since the winter of eighty-two when I had a fortnight's shore leave in Bombay."

"Yes indeed," Beloît agreed. "But we only get to initiate *hommes du nord* once a year, and we got to do it proper." He grinned at Pierre. "Right, La Page?"

Pierre nodded.

"Though it does look," Beloît continued, walking over to Louie, who was sleeping face first on the ground, "like we might have us a dead north man here." He paused to pack his pipe. "What do you think?" he asked, nudging the boy's ribs with the toe of his moccasin. "Is it alive?"

Augustine laughed. "He looks like he's been whipped with a cat-o'-nine-tails and keelhauled."

While the men smoked, Pierre urged Louie to eat. "You've got to take a little food." Pierre remembered how weak he'd been during his first summer with a brigade. "You'll never make it through the day if you don't." He finally persuaded Louie to drink some water and take a few spoonfuls of lukewarm corn.

"What's McHenry got his sights on?" La Petite rose from his seat at the base of a white pine. The commander was standing on a bare rock, staring at the horizon. Pierre followed La Petite to the shore.

La Petite asked McHenry, "Fire?"

McHenry nodded. "By that smoke plume I'd say it's a right big blaze."

Pierre saw a thin yellow wisp above the horizon.

"Should I get your glass?" La Petite asked. The commander carried a small brass telescope in a varnished box.

"No need," Mc Henry said. "We'll just have to keep our eyes on the wind. It hasn't rained in some places since May, and fires have been burning off and on all summer."

"Any big ones?" La Petite asked.

"I heard that a hundred square miles of timber have gone up already."

La Petite whistled softly as the three of them stared at the distant smoke trail.

Later that same morning, Pierre's brigade met an XY Company crew at Wooden Horse Falls portage. The XY traders had just unloaded their canoes and were getting ready to make the carry.

Though Commander McHenry hailed the group with a civil, "Morning, gentlemen," he received only sneers in return.

Beloît jumped in. "Are you Potties lost out here in the big woods?" Potties was an insulting nickname. "You're a long way from your mamas' laps."

Curses flew between the groups.

In the middle of the ruckus Beloît shouted, *"Je suis l'homme."*

That brought a broad-shouldered XY man forward, who said, "Any pig can squeal. How about backing up that mouth with a little contest?"

"Name it," Beloît snapped.

"Would a race from here"—he paused— "to Saganaga Lake be too much for you?"

"Done."

The Norwesters scrambled to unload. A pair of men shouldered each canoe, while the rest, double-packed, headed up the trail. Pierre would have enjoyed pausing to view the rapids if he'd had time. A white funnel of foam roared through a bare chasm of rock, and at the falls there was a sudden three-stage drop where the water fell thirty feet into a roiling pool.

It took several trips to haul all the goods across the portage, and the brigades taunted each other the whole time. When Beloît and Bellegarde were carrying their canoe and an XY man failed to yield, Beloît yelled, "Get out of my way, Pottie boy."

The XY man tossed down his packs and turned to fight, but McHenry intervened. "I'll dock a month's pay from any man who raises his fists," he said. Beloît spat and continued on his way.

Since the XY brigade had a head start, they began their last carry ahead of the Norwesters. La Petite led the final group up the trail, followed closely by Pierre and Louie. Though La Petite was carrying three packs, the boys still had to jog to keep up with his mammoth strides.

On the top of the last ridge La Petite suddenly stopped. Pierre plowed into him, and Louie, who was following close behind, tripped over Pierre's feet and crashed to the ground.

La Petite shouted a curse.

For a moment Pierre thought La Petite was yelling at him and Louie. Then he saw the boulder. The last group of XY men had rolled a huge rock into the middle of the trail and piled several windfall logs across the path further ahead.

"Of all the low-down, scum-sucking dogs," the big man

growled. "In all my living days, I never—" Still cursing, he threw down his packs and began clearing the debris. Even with Pierre and Louie's help, there was soon a backup of angry *voyageurs*.

When they finally made their way to the shore of the Granite River, anger turned to outrage. Someone had caved in the bow of one of their canoes with a cannonball-size rock. Though the XY brigade was already out of sight and Wooden Horse Falls was roaring in the background, Beloît bellowed a curse down the lake.

"Save your strength," McHenry said, studying the damaged canoe. It was clearly beyond repair. "La Petite."

"Aye, sir."

"We'll take your canoe and make an express run to Saganaga. Those north shore Ojibwe still make canoes, don't they?"

"Near as I know."

"It will cost us dearly, no doubt, but we have no choice," McHenry said. Then, thinking ahead, he continued, "We'll need two parcels of trade goods and a keg of rum. Let's take two—no, make it four—extra paddlers to bring the new boat back."

Pierre was glad when La Petite signaled for him to come along. He was impressed by the commander's decisiveness. Though McHenry normally let his foreman manage things, he was clearly in charge now. As soon as they were ready to leave, he turned and gave one last order: "You fellows see that the freight is ready to load as soon as we get back."

Pierre was amazed at the speed of the north canoe. Without freight it rode nearly a foot higher in the water, and with two extra paddlers in both the bow and the stern, it skimmed down the Granite River like a ship under sail.

Tight-lipped, the *voyageurs* paddled without their usual jokes and songs. To Pierre, the silence made the river cold and lonely. Usually McHenry consulted charts and notebooks while a canoe was under way, but today he took up a paddle and helped.

The men trotted over one short portage and *saulted,* or shot, two rapids that they never would have tried in a loaded canoe. "Pull hard," Beloît hollered at the head of the Siskile and later the Mariboo rapids, allowing La Petite time to turn the boat carefully straight downstream. Time stopped as their blades whirled above the white water and the canoe shot down. It was easy for Pierre to see how the Granite River got its name. On both sides sheer granite walls, unbroken except for a few mossy ledges that harbored pale clumps of lichens and stunted pines, rose up to block all but a tiny window of sky.

As McHenry predicted, the Ojibwe band on Saganaga bartered hard, demanding a full keg of rum and an assortment of goods for a north canoe. Though McHenry tried to talk them into accepting just trade goods, the Indians were set on rum.

"I hate the liquor trade," he said. Pierre's commander had said the same thing the previous year. "But the more the rum kills them, the more they want it. The cycle has got us all trapped."

It was late afternoon by the time they made it back to Wooden Horse Falls. Pierre assumed that the brigade would soon camp for the night, but the men had other plans.

The *voyageurs* paddled with the energy of men possessed. They remained silent and kept their eyes fixed downstream. No one hummed or even whistled.

It was past sunset when the crew reached Saganaga Lake. Pierre's arms ached, and his right hand was a cramped claw after pulling so long on his paddle. His soreness reminded him of the blisters that had plagued him the summer before. He was glad they would soon stop for the night.

But the brigade struck straight off across the lake. "How long is Saganaga?" Pierre turned and asked La Petite.

"Six miles or so," La Petite said, undaunted by the gathering darkness. "The grand thing about this lake is the islands. A friend of mine counted two hundred of them before he gave up."

"It looks like we're going to see exactly zero on this trip," Pierre replied.

The canoes paddled toward the last pale streaks of purple that lit the western horizon. Last summer Pierre had learned to "trick" away his work by dreaming about other things, but in the dark it was hard to think of anything but his sore hands. Would they ever stop?

"I hope you know how to steer by the stars," Pierre said, as he searched the moonless sky.

"As long as I can see the North Star and the Dipper," La Petite said in a low voice, as if he were afraid to disturb the stillness, "I can navigate all the way to Hudson's Bay."

An hour later the brigade rounded a long point, and Beloît suddenly stopped paddling. He called back in a hoarse whisper, "There they are."

Everyone held his paddle still. Pierre stared down the bay. At the far end of the lake—perhaps two miles away— a campfire flickered.

"Now we got 'em," La Petite growled. Pierre shivered. So the men intended to get back at the XY Company! But what would they do? Murder the fellows in their sleep?

McHenry's canoe drifted alongside La Petite's. "Shall we take that campsite in the south bay?" La Petite asked.

"You're not planning a nighttime visit to our XY friends, are you?" By McHenry's voice, Pierre could tell he was smiling.

"It is a fine evening to go calling, sir."

"Tell me no more," McHenry replied, shifting to his commander's voice. "But I must warn you that McTavish wants no more bloodshed."

"Aye, sir," La Petite answered. "But first we'll have a little supper."

After paddling back around the point and out of sight,

Bellegarde cooked the men a quick meal. They ate fast and dispensed with their usual bragging and storytelling. Later, as they sat pulling on their little clay pipes under the broad, starlit sky, La Petite suddenly said, "Listen."

At first Pierre could hear nothing. Then he caught the distant sound of singing. Beloît's devilish face, lit by the embers of the fire, broke into a grin. "Just as I hoped. They're celebrating."

La Petite nodded. "They'll be sleeping heavy tonight." He turned to Pierre. "You want to help us pay those Potties a little visit?"

As tired as he was, Pierre was curious. "Sure." He nodded, but even as he agreed, he wondered if it was wise to go along.

McHenry rose and said, "Good night." He bent down to light a candle in the coals of the fire, then walked toward his tent. Just before he closed the flap, he said, "Take care of yourselves, lads."

Pierre studied the distorted shadows that danced across the tent wall as McHenry set his candle down, reached into his book crate, and settled back for his nightly ritual.

"Reading," Beloît snorted. "If that ain't a waste of good candles."

Two hours later a single canoe headed up the lake toward the XY camp. The fire they'd noticed earlier had burned down to a dim orange dot. They carried a half dozen rifles. "Pack one for each man, just in case," La Petite had said. Beloît brought a single pack sack and stowed it in the bow.

As they neared the other camp, Pierre tried to stay calm. What if the XY men awoke? Beloît would have no qualms about using his gun. Two traders had been murdered by XY men last spring. Imagine his mother's face when she found out he'd been shot during a midnight raid on a rival camp!

From a hundred yards offshore Pierre could hear snoring. "This is going to be too easy," Beloît whispered loudly. La Petite shushed him.

Using hand signals, the men paddled around to the back side of the island and crept ashore. Beloît opened his pack and whispered, "This little gimlet should do the trick." He pulled out a little tee-handled drill. Next he drew out a pistol and shoved it into the red sash at his waist.

La Petite shook his head and said, "No, Jean," but Beloît only patted the handle and said, "Just in case—"

Still shaking his head, La Petite followed him into the darkness with Pierre close behind.

Their moccasins were quiet as they crept over the mossy ground toward the enemy camp. When they got within sight of the campfire, they dropped to their knees. The loud snores of the XY men hinted that they'd celebrated as hard as Beloît had hoped.

When Beloît saw the rum kegs, he grinned so widely that Pierre could see his dirty teeth shining in the starlight. Though a man was sleeping under a canoe only two yards away, Beloît was calm. Handing a keg to La Petite and Pierre, he motioned for them to pass it on. One by one the men relayed the kegs back into the shadows. Pierre's heart raced each time an XY man rolled over in his sleep or sighed. If someone shouted an alarm, the odds would be four to one against them.

In a few minutes they had carried ten kegs into the quiet of the woods. There Beloît knelt with a soft chuckle. "We'll take one for ourselves, and I'll fix the rest good," he said. Grinning, he bored a hole in each keg with his gimlet. As the liquor trickled out onto the ground, Beloît laughed, and La Petite had to cuff his head to quiet him.

When the job was finally done, the men started back to their canoe. But Beloît said, "Wait."

Everyone stopped, and La Petite waved his hand and said, "Let's go, Jean."

"We've got to stack them back up."

"What?" La Petite whispered.

"Can't you see what a great joke it will be?" Beloît insisted. "They'll get up in the morning, thinking everything is normal, but when they go to load their rum—"

"All right, all right," La Petite whispered to quiet him.

Pierre's heart was pounding harder than ever as they relayed the kegs back into place. The XY men were sleeping more fitfully now, and it was only a matter of time before someone woke up.

Beloît was setting the last keg in place when an XY man sat up and mumbled, "What's that?" Before the poor fel-

51

low could say another word, Beloît pulled out his pistol and clubbed him on the side of the head. Then, catching the unconscious man by the shoulders, he laid him quietly back on his blanket.

The entire crew froze. Pierre waited for someone else to sit up or shout. Across the fire a man coughed, and another rolled over. Pierre was sure that someone would hear his heart pounding, but the ragged snoring continued.

It's got to be the rum, Pierre thought as his crew began crawling back toward the shelter of the woods. When Pierre reached the shadows, he heard a dull, scratching sound. He turned, amazed to see Beloît drilling a hole in the bottom of an XY canoe. Pierre looked at La Petite, who shrugged and motioned for the men to move on.

As soon as they got their canoe into the water, La Petite handed each man a rifle. A battle looked inevitable. A few minutes later, there was a rustling in the underbrush. Pierre heard a rifle cock to his left, and he lifted his own gun to his shoulder.

Pierre saw a shadowy figure at the edge of the woods. A second rifle cocked in the dark. Pierre was feeling for the trigger of his own gun when a voice croaked, *"Je suis l'homme."* Then he saw Beloît's ugly grin.

As the men lowered their rifles, Pierre heard La Petite mumble, "Can you believe that?" Beloît waved the XY commander's plumed top hat above his head.

When Beloît reached the men, he declared, "I got no use for fancy hats, but these are some real fine feathers."

He set the elegant top hat on the ground and placed his fat moccasin on the crown. Crushing it flat, he pulled the elegant ostrich plumes from the band and sailed the hat out over the dark lake. Long after the splash, Beloît was still enjoying a wicked chuckle.

CHAPTER 6

Night Journey

As they paddled back up the lake, the water sparkled with starlight, and a thin slip of moon hung like a slender beacon above the black shore. The quiet reminded Pierre of a night the previous spring when he and his father had speared northern pike in a little stream near their house. In an hour they'd filled half a washtub with fish and were ready to start home. "There's no sense wasting lamp oil," Father had said.

When Father turned the wick down, the world went totally black. Then as Pierre's eyes adjusted, the moonlight gradually illuminated the woods and the dew-flecked fields beyond.

Now, with the excitement over, Pierre felt the effects of

the all-day paddle. He was looking forward to a sound sleep. But when they returned to the North West camp, the canoes were all loaded.

"What's going on, La Petite?" Pierre asked. Was the moonlight tricking his eyes?

"We can't stop now," La Petite said. "We've got to put some distance between us and those Potties before they wake up."

"What?" Pierre said. He couldn't believe his ears.

"We've got to get clear of Saganaga tonight."

Augustine, who was sitting just ahead of Pierre, turned and said, "He's right, mate. If we tried to paddle past that island after daybreak, we'd be eating musket balls for breakfast."

The brigade struck out across the lake. They paddled in silence past the XY camp and never stopped until they portaged into Cypress Lake at noon. Pierre was astonished at the endurance of the men. The day was hot and sunny, and smoke from the big fire that was smoldering south of Saganaga Lake sometimes drifted over the canoes and burned Pierre's eyes. But the old-timers were too busy joking about the XY brigade to care about the heat or the smoke. They'd slept less than four hours in the last day and a half, yet they pulled steadily on their paddles.

"We sure got them Potties, eh, Auggie?" Beloît called to Augustine.

The old sailor grinned, accepting the nickname.

"Though I got to admit I never knew what a Pottie was until yesterday," he said, "I agree that we gave 'em exactly what they deserved."

Beloît threw back his head and laughed, snorting through his deformed nose.

Louie was having a hard time. The aftereffects of the rum, along with the lack of sleep, had left him so sick he could barely sit up to paddle. When Pierre asked him how he was doing, he said, "Death would be an improvement." Though Louie could only manage a single pack on the portages, no one teased him except Beloît.

The more the crewmen took pity on Louie, the more Beloît went out of his way to pick on him. After slogging through Swamp Portage just after dawn, Louie had sat down on a rock to catch his breath. Beloît called to him. "You sure have been quiet today, Noise Box. I appreciate it so much that I got a present for you." The bowman was crouched in knee-high grass and grinning as if he'd found a treasure. Louie walked over, and Beloît picked up a half-rotted muskrat carcass by the tail and dangled it in front of his face.

When Louie turned green and gagged, Beloît feigned surprise. He kept up the same tricks all day long. On Monument Portage he sneaked up behind Louie and goosed him with a wet canoe paddle. During a pipe stop on Little Knife Lake he "accidentally" blew pipe smoke in Louie's face.

"Why don't you leave him be?" Pierre said. He sat down beside Louie and offered him a drink from his tin cup.

"Look," Beloît called, tapping his clay pipe on the side of a tree and letting the ashes fall on Pierre's feet. "Squeaks has found himself a little nursemaid. Isn't that sweet?"

Beloît didn't care if no one else laughed. Though most of the men got quieter as the day went on, Beloît got louder. And the more Pierre tried to protect Louie, the meaner Beloît got. Pierre thought about giving up, but when he remembered how La Londe had helped him last summer, he vowed he'd do the same for Louie.

By midday, Pierre had paddled beyond tiredness. His palms felt as if he'd been holding hot coals. His arms were stiff wooden poles, detached from his body. The closest he'd ever come to being this exhausted had happened last autumn. It was a Saturday morning. He and his father were bucking up firewood with a two-man crosscut—a saw his father called a misery whip—and Pierre was anxious to prove that his first summer as a *voyageur* had made him into a man.

"You ready for a break?" Father had asked, after they'd been going steady for an hour.

"I'm fine," Pierre had replied. So they went on pulling the big saw back and forth, cutting up block after block of wood.

When Father asked, "You tired yet?" Pierre shook his head. Though his hair was plastered to his forehead with sweat and his back ached from crouching over the saw buck, he had to show Father he could match any pace he set.

Pierre could see a steely determination in Father's eyes, and he knew he would be offering no more rests. From now on it would be up to Pierre to call the contest off. The blade ripped back and forth. The sugary scent of green maple burned in Pierre's nostrils as the sawdust piled over the toes of his boots. They lifted a new log into place. The blade started again.

Mother saved them both by calling them to lunch. As sore as Pierre's body was that afternoon, it ached twice as much the next day.

Now Pierre wondered how he would feel after two days and a night of brutal paddling.

In late afternoon they stopped for a smoke halfway up Knife Lake. "Do you suppose we're clear of those XY upstarts by now, Commander?" La Petite called to McHenry as he sculled his long steering paddle in the water and turned his canoe toward shore.

McHenry turned to Beloît before he answered. "How many holes did you bore in that canoe, Jean?"

"A good dozen, sir," Beloît replied.

McHenry smiled. "No doubt they'll have to bargain for a new canoe same as we did. I'd say it's plenty safe to camp here."

"Aye, sir," La Petite replied. "We'll not see those Potties this side of the border."

"Agreed then."

Those words were heaven sent for Pierre. After thirty-six hours without sleep he felt as if he were floating high above the water, looking down on himself. Every sound, from the voices of the crew to the calls of the shore birds and the lapping of the waves against the hull, was miles away.

"Wake up, La Page," Beloît yelled. "You gonna help us make camp? Or you gonna play sick like your little lady friend here?" Startled, Pierre looked up. Beloît had stepped out into the shallow water and was jabbing Louie in the ribs with a paddle. Louie's head was slumped over a pack sack, and all he could do was moan.

Augustine wet a kerchief and sponged off Louie's sunburned neck.

"Ow," Louie groaned.

"I know it hurts," the old sailor said, "but a little cool water will take away the sting. I've gotten scorched a few times myself. The worst time was off the coast of Morocco, when I was about your age. You've had too much grog and too much sun—that's like being hit with a hurricane at high tide."

Even though Beloît called him Little Lou's Mama, Augustine helped the boy out of the canoe.

When Pierre stood up to disembark, he was so stiff that he almost fell backward.

In fifteen minutes the canoes were unloaded and the campfire was lit. Pierre stood for a moment and admired Knife Lake. Their campsite was on a slender point that jutted out from the south shore. Towering white pines offered a canopy that filtered the sunlight to a soft, mottled green. A deep carpet of pine needles, dry from weeks without rain, crunched beneath Pierre's moccasins. A gentle breeze from the west kept the mosquitoes away.

While Bellegarde's soup pot boiled, the men inspected the hulls of their canoes and shared stories of the raid on the XY camp. They regummed the seams with balsam pitch. The bow of Pierre's canoe needed a new length of *wattape,* the root lacing that held the birch bark sheets together.

Long after dinner was done, the members of the raiding party were still laughing and bragging about how they'd showed up those Potties. Beloît was the hero of everyone's story. "Why, after we was done with the rum kegs and ready to turn tail," Augustine said, "Jean Beloît took out his gimlet and riddled one a their boats with holes."

Pierre smiled. He knew the story would get a little better each time it was told. By next spring Beloît would be known as the man who'd single-handedly humiliated an entire XY brigade.

As the fire was dying down to coals, Augustine offered to "pipe a tune" if anyone cared to dance. To Pierre's amazement, a dozen men volunteered. With a tired grin, McHenry retired to his tent.

For once the commander lit no candle. "Looks like our leader is too tired to read tonight," Pierre said to La Petite.

"He may not feel like reading, but he could go another two days without rest if he needed to." When Pierre frowned in disbelief, La Petite continued. "Though Mc-

Henry may not look the part, there's not a tougher man this side of Lake Athabasca."

"But all he does is hide in his tent and read," Pierre said. Pierre loved literature too, but when he saw a pale, bookish fellow like McHenry, he hated to admit it. "He looks like he's spent his whole life locked up in a library."

"Don't let that pasty complexion fool you," La Petite said. "Though he may be a reader, he's a doer, too. When the time comes, you'll see what I mean."

Pierre didn't believe a word of it. If going to college meant he would grow up to be a frail bookworm like McHenry, he wanted no part of it. Forget his mother's dreams of his becoming a doctor or a lawyer. He would spend the rest his life as a canoeman.

CHAPTER 7

Wild Fire

Pierre awoke to the sound of hooves. The Potties are attacking, he thought. But where would they get horses? As his mind shook off the fog of sleep, he tossed his blanket aside and rolled out from under the canoe. The moon was down, and the black-barked pines were twisting in a strong wind that had switched to the southeast.

Puffs of yellow smoke swirled in the predawn light. Pierre stared down the shore. For a moment, he thought he saw a caribou running past McHenry's tent. He rubbed his eyes. There were two more animals, charging out of the woods and leaping into the water. More of the herd followed. All the men were on their feet now. Beloît was leveling his gun on the nearest caribou, when McHenry suddenly shouted, "No, Jean."

The *Jean* sounded strange, since the men rarely called Beloît by his first name, but it got his attention.

"What the—" Beloît protested. "That's a week's worth of meat."

"Listen," McHenry shouted, grabbing Beloît's gun barrel in his hand.

The whole camp was quieted by the urgency in McHenry's voice.

Then Pierre heard the roar of a huge wind, far off but unmistakable.

"It's a crown fire," McHenry hollered. "Load up, men, we've got to get clear of this shore."

Pierre had never been close to a forest fire, but he'd heard stories about updrafts that generated terrific winds. The fire that had been burning south of Saganaga Lake had turned with the wind and was rushing straight for them.

The men loaded their canoes in seconds, heaping the packs, parcels, and kegs in each boat and grabbing their paddles. By the time the crew scrambled into the canoes, the roar of the fire was so loud that McHenry's hollered, "Double time," sounded like a choked whisper.

Along with the clouds of thick, yellow smoke, hot cinders blew out of the pines and hit the men on their backs and arms. The hot ashes were particularly painful, since half the men had been sleeping naked in the heat. Beloît, who was standing in the bow, slapped several hot pine needles off his shoulders without comment, but when a flaming ember landed on his buttocks, he let out a yelp that made them laugh.

Their laughter came to a sudden stop. Just down the shore a squirrel leaped from the crown of a burning pine with a demonlike shriek, its back and tail blazing. Pierre watched in horror as the poor creature hit the lake with a sickening hiss of steam. Next came a raccoon and then a marten. Their eyes were white with fear as they dove into the water.

A moment later the rippling firestorm engulfed the campsite they had occupied only minutes before. The noise was deafening. The men held their paddles and stared openmouthed as an orange tongue of flame, driven by an enormous wind, shot out over the water and rolled skyward. Thick, yellow-gray smoke swirled across the lake as miniature jets of steam rose from the hot embers hitting the water.

Pierre stared at the roaring inferno. Though the water stopped the fire from reaching the men, further down the bay the flames leaped right over a narrow arm of the lake.

"Blessed Mother of God," Pierre heard Louie whisper behind him. He turned and saw the same look of fear and wonder on every face.

"You suppose it's too early for breakfast?" Beloît's voice drowned out the fading din of the fire. "If we're gonna sit around and gawk at this old fire, we might as well be eating." When they looked at him standing naked in the bow, everyone had to laugh. Leave it to Beloît to think of his stomach at a time like this.

CHAPTER 8

Pictographs

The voyageurs stopped on the far end of Knife Lake to sort through their hastily loaded goods. The pale, dirty pink of the sunrise revealed a blackened landscape to the south. Though the wind had shifted to the west, a burned smell lingered in the air. Pierre stared at the devastation. Though most of the trees had been incinerated by the fire, a few green crowns showed that the flames had skipped over some pockets of pine. He was glad that a few of the majestic trees had been spared.

After breakfast the brigade started over the Knife Lake portage. Pierre had just started up the trail when he stepped on a sharp rock and yelled, "Ouch." As he hopped forward to ease the pain, another pointed rock plunged into the ball of his foot. "Ow," he yelled again.

La Petite, walking just behind him, laughed and said, "If you're going to sing so early in the morning, my friend, at least pick a happy song."

From further back Augustine called, "Should I pipe a little tune for you?"

Pierre moaned, "I think I just cut my foot in half."

"They call this Big Knife portage for good reason," La Petite said. "The slates are tipped on edge like knife blades for the whole forty-three rods."

Pierre knew a rod was sixteen feet. At least it would be a short portage.

His moccasins did little to cushion the pain of the carry. I may as well be barefooted, Pierre thought, as his 180-pound load pressed down on his shoulders.

Once they had finished the carry, the brigade made excellent time. They crossed Carp and Birch lakes with favorable winds, and portaged the Great Whitewood Carrying Place—a sweeping curve above a split stream that fell in a series of rushing cascades into Basswood Lake.

As they boarded their canoes and started up Basswood, Commander McHenry took a turn in La Petite's canoe. During the trip he switched from one canoe to another, giving each crew a turn at sharing the burden of an extra passenger. Since the wind was now out of the northwest—the very course they were on—Pierre was not excited about taking extra weight in his canoe. A crate of the commander's books came with him too.

McHenry was seated just ahead of Pierre and Louie. Before they'd taken a dozen paddle strokes, La Petite said, "You know, Commander, young La Page here is quite a scholar."

"Is that so?" McHenry turned and smiled at Pierre.

Pierre blushed as Beloît chortled, "That's right, sir. If he could paddle as well as he can do his schoolwork, we'd be at Rainy River by now." The men laughed at this fine joke.

McHenry ignored Beloît. "Did you go to the Catholic school in Lachine?"

Pierre nodded. He hated being the center of attention. Beloît would tease him unmercifully if he started talking about school!

"Those sisters are a dedicated lot," McHenry said. "You're fortunate to have teachers who love learning. I'll bet you read lots of poetry."

"Yes, sir, we did." Pierre smiled as he thought back to his teacher, Sister André. She urged Pierre to study things deeply and to never be satisfied with simple answers. " 'We are born to inquire after the truth,' " she would often say, quoting the famous Montaigne. She would also quote the Greek philosopher Plato: " 'The life which is unexamined is not worth living.' "

Pierre grinned as he recalled Sister, standing before the class in her gray robe, reciting those lines. She spread her arms and looked, in the words of Pierre's friend Marc, "like a skinny bird about to fly out the window."

Just then the canoes turned into the main part of the lake, and the full force of the wind hit them. Green whitecaps rolled out of the northwest, threatening to swamp any canoe that veered from a straight upwind course. The men feathered their paddles, turning the blades flat into the wind on their forward strokes and pulling back hard through the roiling foam.

"And did you read much Latin poetry?" McHenry ignored the terrific wind.

Pierre nodded, hoping the commander would drop the subject.

But McHenry continued. "How about Horace and Ovid?" he asked.

"Sister loved them both. Last spring we had to memorize a long section of *Metamorphoses* and—"

That was too much for Beloît. "Talk French, you two," he hollered from the bow. "How can a man navigate a canoe with all this silly blabbering about poets?" He spit out the *p* in *poets* as if it were an obscenity.

McHenry chuckled, doffing his tall hat before it could blow off in the wind. "Our gentle bowman is right," he said, "and considering the weather, it might be wise of me to lend a hand."

The commander then slipped off his coat and took up a paddle. Pierre was surprised at how quickly he picked up the rhythm. As Beloît sang, "Pull, pull, pull," from the bow, the commander's muscles rippled beneath his loose white shirt. Though McHenry looked thin and frail, Pierre could sense a whipcord strength in his arms and shoulders.

Paddling hard across the Z-shaped lake, they passed a

Hudson's Bay post on the north side and an Indian village that lay on a long point to the south. There was little talk as the men focused on the waves, holding their blades when the bow rose high on a foaming crest and pulling when the canoe dipped down into a green trough. Everyone but Beloît looked tense. When the wind was at its worst and Pierre was measuring the distance to a nearby island for a possible swim in case they broached, or tipped, broadside in the waves, Beloît laughed and hollered, "Hold on to your hats, *hivernants*."

At last they reached the lee shore of Basswood Lake. Though the crowns of the tall white pines were swaying and creaking in the wind, the rock ledge where they camped was sheltered and quiet. While the men unloaded the canoes, McHenry excused himself. "I'd help you, lads," the commander explained, handing his paddle to Pierre, "but these mitts just can't stand much abuse these days."

Taking the paddle from McHenry, Pierre saw what he meant. The tips of his fingers were a lumpy mass of scar tissue, and his fingernails were cracked and bleeding. At that moment Pierre realized that McHenry usually kept his fingers curled to conceal these scars. This was the first time Pierre had gotten a close look at his hands.

As soon as the commander was out of earshot, Pierre turned to La Petite. "Where did he get those terrible marks on his hands?"

"McHenry?"

Pierre nodded.

"I told you the commander's been through a lot." La Petite handed a pack to Pierre. "You'd better ask him yourself sometime."

Pierre tried to think what could have caused such terrible wounds. An animal bite? An accident with a machine?

Supper was a quiet affair for a change, and as soon as he finished eating, Pierre crawled under the nearest canoe and collapsed onto his blanket. His feet were still sore from the Big Knife Portage, and his body ached as it had the previous summer. As tired as he was, his sleep was fitful.

A tangled dream woke him once during the night. He was standing beside Celeste on the big pier back in Lachine where ships docked to pick up furs and deliver goods to the North West depot. Though it was midday, the pier was empty. Just then a strange canoe floated by. It was painted black and covered with an arched birchbark top like an Ojibwe grave house. As the bow of the canoe turned in the current, Pierre saw Kennewah's body lying still and cold. Her hands were folded across her chest, and her eyes were staring straight up.

"No," Pierre whispered, but when Celeste turned to see what he was staring at, the body had changed. It was no longer Kennewah, but Beloît. When Beloît, pale as a dead man and naked, sat up and grinned, Celeste screamed.

Pierre woke in a cold sweat. The wind was still howling through the pines overhead, and for a moment he couldn't remember where he was. It took him a long time to calm the wild beating of his heart. He rubbed his eyes. As he thought about the hazy line that divided dreams from reality, he was reminded of a quote Sister André had painted on the wall above her blackboard: "We are such stuff as dreams are made on, and our little life is rounded with a sleep."

Pierre breathed in the scent of cold ashes and pine needles. He tried to clear the picture of Kennewah from his mind, but for the remainder of that night, there was no way to escape the cold vacancy of her eyes.

The calm weather continued through the next few days, and the brigade took advantage of the perfect conditions. Rising early and paddling hard, they made great time.

Before breakfast the men took the Great Pine and Wheelbarrow portages. In the purple haze of dawn, the Basswood River was a thundering cataract, surging over rugged outcroppings of granite that were streaked with white and rose quartz. It was high summer, and the whole of the north was bursting with life. The rocky paths were bordered by bright green clumps of bunch-berries, delicate ferns, and feathery ground pines. War-blers and thrushes bobbed through the undergrowth, while jays and nuthatches flitted through the branches overhead.

Three miles into Crooked Lake the brigade paddled

past a tall granite cliff that was streaked with many colors. As they drew closer, Pierre noticed shapes painted on the rocks. "Look, La Petite," he said, "a picture of a moose and a canoe filled with men."

"That it is," he replied, as the men shipped their paddles and went into a silent glide. "It looks like a war canoe. And see there beside it—a sun, a human hand, and a crane, too."

Pierre admired the rich red and yellow tones of the artwork. Each picture was drawn at the height a man could reach while standing in a canoe.

"Who would ever go to all the trouble?" Louie asked.

"And where did they get the paint?" Pierre added, studying the subtle colorations. The figures were stiff and flat, but they were strong and filled with meaning.

"No one knows," La Petite said. "They've been here as long as anyone—either Indian or white—can recall."

"I've heard," McHenry said from the trailing canoe, "that they used iron oxide and some sort of fish oil." Pierre studied some of the weirder shapes. There was a man with horns curling up from his head, a sea monster, a strange disk shape, and a mischievous gnomelike face.

What sort of people had lived on this lake? Were these pictures of their gods? Their hopes? Their dreams?

"The one thing we know for sure," La Petite said, nodding upward, "is that those are Sioux arrows up there."

Pierre tipped his head back. At least two dozen arrows protruded from a tiny cleft near the top of the cliff.

"According to the story," La Petite said, "a Sioux war party came through this country and left those arrows as a warning to the Ojibwe that they might return at any time."

"It was probably the same bunch of Sioux that butchered La Vérendrye's party up on Massacre Island," Beloît put in. "But let's not waste the whole day jabbering. Paddle!"

"Aye, aye, sir," Augustine joked, and the crew all laughed as they took up their paddles again.

The brigade pushed steadily inland. The weather was so hot that the men paddled bare chested, and Beloît dressed in what he called Indian style, wearing only a breechclout and his dirty red cap.

"You hoping to be adopted by some rich Ojibwe chief?" La Petite asked.

"Je suis l'homme," Beloît shot back. "If he's lucky, maybe I'll adopt him."

The only incident to mar their trip occurred at the Curtain Falls portage. Pierre was walking just ahead of Beloît and Louie, who were carrying a north canoe. Louie slipped on a moss-covered rock and yelled. Though Beloît managed to keep the canoe from sliding over the ledge, Louie fell.

Beloît and Pierre ran to the edge of the trail. The black waters below were still and empty. Pierre could hear the roar of the falls downstream. Had Louie drowned? Last summer his friend La Londe had perished just as suddenly.

Beloît said, "Look," and pointed to a rock ledge about twenty feet below. Louie was lying on an outcropping above the water. He wasn't moving and his left arm was folded under his body, but Pierre prayed that he was alive. Pierre could already see the company courier, hat in hand, delivering the news to Louie's mother that her son was never coming home.

Pierre, Marc, Maurice, and Beloît climbed down the cliff, careful not to dislodge any rocks and finish what the fall hadn't. When they got to Louie he was unconscious, and there was a cut above his right eye, but he was breathing deeply and evenly. "That's a good sign," Beloît said, as they lifted him onto a blanket and gingerly carried him back up the hillside.

They laid him in the shade of a big spruce, and as soon as McHenry dabbed some cold water on Louie's forehead, his eyes flashed open. "What—" Louie faltered. "What hit me?"

His confusion worried Pierre, but by the time the rest of the brigade had finished the portage, Louie was already sitting up. He grinned weakly at Pierre and said, "I'll bet you thought you were going to have to dig a grave?"

"Lie down and rest," Pierre said.

When Louie obeyed, the commander took Pierre aside. "With a blow to the head like that, it's important that you don't let him fall asleep."

Pierre sat beside Louie until nightfall, telling his friend stories and reciting silly poems until McHenry finally said that it was safe to let him rest.

By the next morning, Louie was back to his old chattering self. "Noise Box," Beloît shouted, "if you don't pipe down, I'm gonna to take you back to that cliff and throw you off again."

CHAPTER 9

Crane Lake Fort

Two days later McHenry's brigade reached the North West Company fort at Crane Lake. They were greeted by a volley of shouts, and as they neared the shore, a grizzled fellow stepped through the gate and discharged an ancient musket skyward. With a toothless grin the old man watched his load of grapeshot rain down on the men and canoes like a sudden hailstorm.

"Now that's what I call a fine hello," Beloît said.

After talking a moment, the men unloaded their canoes. Pierre had just finished his second trip to the fort when he caught the black sheen of a girl's hair out of the corner of his eye.

"Kennewah," Pierre called. "Kenne—" He stopped as a pretty Ojibwe girl turned toward him. She smiled.

Pierre lowered his eyes. It was so easy to forget that Kennewah and her whole family were gone.

"What you squealing at, La Page?" Beloît snarled.

"Nothing," Pierre replied, digging the toe of his moccasin into the sandy path.

"Well, let's finish unloading. It's your turn to haul that damned box of books."

Pierre lifted McHenry's crate to his shoulder and hurried toward the front gate.

After a two-day stop at the fort, McHenry split his brigade into two groups. One group headed north to Quetico Lake, while McHenry took Pierre's party south to Lake Vermilion. Pierre hoped McHenry would send Beloît north with the other group, but the commander kept the crews in each canoe intact. At least La Petite and Louie would be going with him.

The Vermilion River emptied into Crane only a few hundred yards from the fort at a rugged rapids called the Chute. Here the brigade made a predawn carry to start the thirty-mile river journey.

The Chute was a white funnel of foam that roared between two huge, rounded boulders. "Just last month," La Petite said, raising his voice over the rushing water, "they said a fellow slipped as he was stepping out of his canoe up there. One of his mates made a grab for him, but it was too late. When they found the body, his face looked like he'd dived into a brickyard."

Pierre shuddered as he studied the powerful white funnel. A single misstep was all it took. At the head of the rapids Pierre saw a freshly painted paddle blade, tied in the shape of a cross to mark the death.

At sunrise the brigade encountered a spectacular stretch of water called the Gorge. Here the portage trail ran high above a deep chasm. Funneled between sheer rock walls, the water rushed over black boulders and ledges. In places the path was only half a step from the cliff's edge. Thinking back to Louie's near tragedy at Curtain Falls, Pierre watched his footing carefully.

Beloît teased him at a pose halfway through the carry. "This would be a perfect place for a little cliff diving, eh?" He elbowed Pierre in the ribs and pushed him toward the edge. "The trick is to not kiss any rocks." When Pierre's eyes got big, Beloît gave his usual horselaugh. "I'm only joshing, bookworm."

Above the gorge the current slowed. The river was low and marshy with wild rice beds lining both banks for long stretches. Once, as the canoes cut past a high point of land, an osprey dove off a pine snag and grabbed a fish out of the river only ten feet in front of their bow. Beloît didn't see the bird until it hit the water, and he let out a high-pitched "Eeeh."

As the osprey beat its wings to lift the fish, water splashed in Beloît's face, and the crew roared. "Who's the little woman squealing in the bow?" La Petite called.

"Call her Millie," Augustine said. "She sure is an ugly one."

"Shut yer yaps," Beloît yelled. "I thought we was being attacked."

"Attacked?" Augustine laughed again. "Those birds can really be scary. Just think if it had been a giant woodpecker, Jean. He'd a gone right after your paddle."

"Or maybe his wooden head?" Pierre offered, and the whole crew roared.

"Paddle!" Beloît said. For once he was at a loss for words.

The further they paddled upriver, the more dramatic the landscape became. Other than Table Rock Falls, which required a milelong carry, the portages were easy. The quiet bays were dotted with yellow and white water lilies that gave off a heady scent. Once, when they cut close to a rocky headland, Pierre caught the warm smell of blueberries.

McHenry said, "This country reminds me of the pastoral poetry of Lucretius. Do you know his work, La Page?"

"Not that sissy talk again," Beloît crowed.

Pierre blushed. He'd studied Lucretius but he shook his head.

"Thank the Lord for small favors," Beloît said.

Twice the canoes startled deer at the river's edge, but the animals disappeared into the woods before Beloît could get his gun up.

"Millie," Augustine teased, "is not so quick today. Do you suppose that big bird scared her?"

Beloît grumbled to himself but made no comment.

Pierre enjoyed the wildlife along the river. Red squirrels chattered high in the pines and ran along the bank to scold the canoemen. Ducks quacked in the green rice beds, tipping their tails skyward as they scoured the bottom for food. And birds sang in constant counterpoint to the *chansons* of the crew.

But what excited the *voyageurs* most was the many beaver houses. Piled high with fresh aspen cuttings and mud, the huge beaver lodges hinted that they would have a fine winter's trading ahead. More than once La Petite whistled softly to himself and said, *"Sacre bleu,* this is rich country."

When the brigade reached Lake Vermilion on the following afternoon, they found a perfect campsite in the very first bay. A sand beach—rare in that rocky country—stretched for a hundred yards to the west. A ring of blackened stones showed that many campfires had been made here over the years, and the bare frames of some abandoned wigwams revealed that an Ojibwe band had recently occupied these shores.

"We may as well camp here, gentlemen," McHenry said, reviewing the map that he'd spread across his knees. "It's a good fifteen miles yet to Windigo Point."

"Aye, sir," La Petite replied.

After supper that night McHenry sat longer than usual with the men. Pierre could tell that everyone was glad to be nearing the place where they would build their trading post. La Petite had finished telling about a winter he'd spent at Cumberland House, when Louie asked how far Cumberland was from York Factory. La Petite deferred to

McHenry, saying, "You know that country, sir. What would you guess the distance to be?"

McHenry, uneasy at being the center of attention, replied, "Close to five hundred miles, I believe," as he got up to retire to his tent.

But Louie stopped McHenry by asking, "Is that the country where you got your hands scarred, sir?"

"No, son." McHenry smiled. "That happened back on Lake Champlain years and years ago."

Louie then asked the question that had long been on Pierre's mind: "What sort of accident was it?"

"It wasn't an accident at all," McHenry said. Resigned to telling his story, he stepped back toward the fire. "I was only fifteen at the time and out duck hunting by myself when a Mohawk band ambushed me. A Mohawk woman who'd just lost her son adopted me, and I lived with her family for over a year. They treated me fair enough and helped me learn the customs of the tribe, but I still wasn't much better than a slave. One night I escaped with an Algonquin fellow they'd captured in a raid. We didn't get far before they tracked us down. They killed that Algonquin on the spot, but a fellow who'd hated me all along had bigger plans for me. He tied me to a tree, and started things off by driving a red-hot sword through my foot." McHenry winced involuntarily.

"Next they pulled out my fingernails one at a time— each one more slowly than the next. And as if that wasn't enough, they shoved my bloody fingertips into a bucket of raw coals. Finally . . . they told the children to chew my fingers off." McHenry held his deformed fingertips out toward the firelight, and Pierre shuddered at the pain he must have felt.

"But just when I thought I was a goner, my adopted mother came along, threw her arms around me, and pleaded for them to stop. For a moment I was afraid they were going to harm her, too, but they didn't. A year later I escaped for good."

The men sat in silence. Even Beloît made no jokes. So all the stories Pierre had heard about McHenry were true. Pierre stared at the weird scars on the commander's fingers.

"Enough of this dark talk," McHenry finally said. "Where's your pipe, Augustine? It's time we celebrate our arrival at Vermilion."

"Here, sir," Augustine replied, reaching into his pack. And in a moment the *voyageurs* were dancing to an old French folk tune.

Just before dawn the next morning Pierre was lying half-awake when a loon called. He got up from his blanket and walked to the shore. Though the sky was still gray from the big fire that was burning back at Saganaga, a soft pink light filled the eastern sky. The pungent scent of pine mingled with a warm, marshy smell that drifted up from the river. Though the Vermilion River had been a brownish color, the waters of Lake Vermilion were as clear as snowmelt.

Pierre watched the mother loon swim along the shore, less than twenty feet away. The water was so still that a perfect V wake trailed out from her body. Behind her swam eight fluff-ball babies with tiny wakes of their own. When a man up in the camp coughed, the baby loons shot forward and dove under their mother's wing.

Pierre smiled. He loved the quiet of the morning. Back home his sisters stayed in bed as long as they could, but Pierre liked to get up early. In the summer he'd walk along the shore of the St. Lawrence River. But no matter how early he rose, there was no escaping the sounds of the city: a clattering wagon, a barking dog, a mast creaking on a moored ship. Here was the pure silence of a world untouched by men and their machines.

Knowing they had a short paddle today, the crew woke well after sunrise. They even tidied themselves up a bit, since they would be bartering for a site to build their winter post. Augustine shaved his head with special care, and a few of the men borrowed combs from a pack of trade goods to smooth their wild locks. "What you prettying yourselves up for, fellows?" Beloît asked. "A pig in a poke is still a pig, you know."

They boarded their canoes and set a leisurely pace up a slender bay that opened gradually into the main body of Vermilion. Ahead Pierre saw a few rocky islands and an opening that hinted of bigger waters. "To the west lies

Muskego Point"—La Petite waved his hand toward the pale green shore—"and further on is an Ojibwe village at Wakemup Bay."

By midmorning it was stifling hot, and swarms of horseflies were buzzing low over both canoes. As Pierre paddled, the sweat ran down his bare back and arms. When Louie complained about the heat, La Petite said, "Enjoy the sunshine while you can, Half-pint. Summer only lasts a few weeks this far north. Some years it hardly comes at all."

"I'd sooner see a blizzard than this blasted heat," Louie insisted.

Beloît laughed from the bow. "Don't never say such things. I've seen it snow in August up here."

"You're joking," Louie scoffed.

"Before you know it, you'll be up to your ears in snow-drifts and begging for spring to come."

Pierre watched Louie shrug. It was clear he didn't believe the old-timers.

The brigade worked its way through a winding channel called Oak Narrows and stopped for breakfast on an island where Beloît claimed the Ojibwe sometimes found gold nuggets. "They call this Gold Island for good reason," he said. "I met a brave up on the Maligne River one summer who had a fat lump of gold dangling from a rawhide necklace. He claimed he found that nugget right here."

Pierre looked at the small, rocky island. Other than a

handful of white pines, the land was covered with straggly ferns and a few stunted oaks.

Augustine knelt and scraped a clump of moss aside, revealing a bluish rock that was streaked with sparkling swirls of white. "There's quartz here," he said. "That's gold-bearing rock for sure. But how a man could ever get it out of this granite would be another story."

Ignoring Augustine, Beloît continued. "I warned the fellow not to wear a big nugget like that, but he said, 'It's my *manitou*. It gives me special protection.' Later that week someone slit his throat in his sleep." Beloît paused and whispered, "Some protection."

Surprised by the sympathetic tone in Beloît's voice, Pierre turned toward him. But by then Beloît's eyes were lit by an evil glitter. "Just like that." He chuckled darkly and drew his finger across his throat. "There's no magic that can save a man from cold steel." Then he poked Pierre and Louie in the ribs, adding, "Ain't that right, sweethearts?"

As the day drew on, they paddled past long green islands and towering pines that stood rooted in rock ledges bare of all but the merest trace of soil, and they passed boulder-strewn points, where raucous gulls gathered to nap in the noonday sun. But try as he could to focus on the land and water around him, Pierre couldn't shake from his mind the image of the dead man's necklace. Once when he felt the needle prick of a fly bite on his neck, he wondered if the man had still been alive to feel the pain when the thief ripped the rawhide off his neck.

* * *

Shortly after their afternoon pipe stop, McHenry looked up from his map and announced, "If we cut through that channel, Windigo Point should be straight ahead."

Despite the heat, the commander pulled on his long coat. "Well, gentlemen," he said, adjusting his tall hat, "I'd better get on my meeting clothes if we're going to negotiate our winter lodgments."

The men nodded, and La Petite started a song: *"La belle Lisette, chantait l'autre jour . . ."*

Pierre joined in. He wondered what sort of reception the local band would give them. The Ojibwe on the main canoe routes were used to dealing with the French, but Pierre's father had warned him that the more isolated tribes could be suspicious of traders. "If you treat them right, they'll treat you right," he advised, "but beware if you don't."

Windigo Point was heavily timbered with a mixture of birch and pine and maple. It was four or five miles long, and a series of three small islands protected its north side. As they drew near, Pierre could see a circle of fire-blackened stones in a sandy cove, shielded by the largest and the easternmost of the three islands. A group of children was playing along the shore where several well-worn paths led into the forest.

A little girl was the first to notice the approaching canoes. When she called out, more people soon appeared.

By the time the canoes reached the sandy beach, several dozen Ojibwe had gathered to greet the men.

The peacefulness of the scene impressed Pierre. Unlike the rowdy camp back at Grand Portage, which was always filled with shouts and yapping dogs and even gunshots, this sun-drenched shore was quiet.

As McHenry climbed out of the canoe, Pierre caught the smell of birch smoke and roast venison. A man stepped forward. He wore a breechclout, moccasins, and tight leggings that extended from his ankles to his knees. He was more than six feet tall, and when he raised his hand in greeting, the muscles in his forearm rippled.

"My name is Rat's Liver," he said in French. His hair was cut straight across his forehead, while double braids hung loosely down his back. "I am the chief of the Vermilion band." His profile reminded Pierre of a hawk. Though his dark eyes stared directly at McHenry, his face gave no hint of emotion.

"I am William McHenry," the commander began. "You speak excellent French."

"The missionaries at Sault Ste. Marie taught me, as I have taught my own son, Red Loon." He paused and gestured toward a boy to his right who looked to be about Pierre's age. "I was orphaned when I was only five, and the people at the mission raised me. When I was nine, an aunt from the Vermilion band brought me to this lake."

"You've done well," McHenry said. "We have come from twice as far as the Sault. Our home is a city called

Lachine near Montréal. It is our hope to build a trading post here on your shores."

"Before we talk business," Rat's Liver said, "I must tell you of a dream I had."

"Of course." McHenry nodded respectfully.

"It came to me last night, as clear as a face in the noonday sun. I saw two canoes that looked just like these two you now paddle. In the first canoe rode a man who looked very much like you. He wore a fine blue coat. It had long tails and buttons of bright brass just like these." Rat's Liver touched a button on the commander's coat as he spoke. "The man in that dream took off his coat and gave it to me as a gift. I told him it was far too generous, but he insisted."

Beloît whispered, "He's a smart one."

McHenry's cheeks flushed as he took off his coat and offered it to the chief. Rat's Liver thanked McHenry. Then he put the coat on over his bare chest and turned to his people with a smile. The Ojibwe gathered around the chief and touched the fine-spun cloth.

"Perhaps we can now talk of a proper place for—" McHenry began, but the chief cut him off.

"Thank you, William McHenry. But it is best that we discuss these matters tomorrow. For now, I suggest you camp on the island. There is a fine site on the western end."

Then the chief was gone. As McHenry turned, he winked at Pierre. Pierre frowned and walked back toward his canoe. Why was the commander winking? After pad-

dling all these weeks, they were being sent off to an island like disobedient children, yet he was grinning as if
he'd just played a clever trick.

The men were silent over supper, and McHenry retired
to his tent without a word of his plans for the next day.
Later, as Pierre turned restlessly in his blankets, he was
furious with McHenry. The campsite the chief had recom-
mended was hot and mosquito infested. Though the men
heaped green leaves on the fire to make a smudge, it did
little good. Had the commander read so many books that
he'd addled his brain? What would the fellow do tomorrow? Make the chief a present of their canoes?

CHAPTER 10

Windigo Point

The men woke up grumpy. The air was stagnant, and clouds of mosquitoes hummed all around them. "I've never seen 'em this big," Beloît grumbled, crushing a bug in his fist and slapping his hand against his thigh as he spoke. "I swear there's enough meat on these fellows to make stew."

"Let's not exaggerate, Jean," McHenry said from the doorway of his tent. "This is going to be grand country for our trading post."

"And how do you figure on getting the land to build your post?" Beloît asked. "You gonna trade your pants?"

Though the crew laughed, Pierre could see real worry in their faces. Everyone knew that if McHenry proved to be a poor leader, they would have no chance for a successful trading season.

* * *

Shortly after breakfast, McHenry announced, "It's time to call on our neighbors." Dressed in gray knee breeches and a white linen shirt with puffy sleeves, McHenry looked totally out of place in the wilderness. Except for his scraggly, uncombed hair, he could have been a courtier preparing for an audience with a king.

Leaving the freight and three men behind on the island, the crew paddled a single canoe back to the Ojibwe village. As they neared the beach, a large, wolflike dog ran to the water's edge and barked once. "I'll bet he'd make a fine sled dog," Bellegarde said, and the crewmen nodded.

Pierre could see that there was a bigger crowd gathered today. Along with the chief and several men and boys, there were a dozen women. They wore deerskin dresses that were decorated with delicate white beading and soft colored grasses. They approached the shore with lowered eyes, their children clinging to their sides. How different these ladies looked from the Indian women at Grand Portage, who wore layers of cheap calico, put brass rings on their arms, and tied sleigh bells around their ankles.

Rat's Liver greeted McHenry as the commander stepped from his canoe. The chief was dressed in McHenry's coat, and he was smiling. "*Bonjour,* William McHenry," Rat's Liver began. "Welcome once again to Windigo Point. I would like to—"

"If you'll excuse me, Chief," McHenry interrupted. Everyone turned toward the commander, astonished at his rudeness. "But I must tell you of a wondrous dream that I had this very night."

This had better be good, Pierre thought, studying the angry eyes of the chief. "The vision came to me as clear as the light of this fine morning." McHenry paused to wave his hand toward the eastern sky. "In my dream I arrived on a point that looked very much like this one, and I was greeted by a noble brave who looked remarkably like you. In fact, he was wearing a blue coat, just like the one you now have on. And when I reached out in my dream to shake his hand, he offered my brigade a fine piece of land on which to build a trading post."

Rat's Liver's face was stern as he contemplated the commander's words. Finally the chief spoke slowly. "This is a powerful vision, William McHenry," he said, touching the commander's shoulder. "I will show you a place worthy of such a dream."

"Haw, haw." Beloît laughed, startling both McHenry and the chief, who were just reaching out to shake hands. Then, to Pierre's astonishment, Beloît clapped Rat's Liver on the shoulder and said, "He sure got you there, didn't he, Chief?"

Would they all be killed? Surely Beloît had gone too far this time. But he wasn't done. He turned to Rat's Liver's son, Red Loon, and tousled his hair. "Looks like the talking's done, Loon Boy," he said. "Would you happen to know of any unattached *mesdemoiselles* in these parts?"

Shocked, Red Loon opened his mouth to speak, but

Beloît cut him off. "Now, there's a gal to match a bold man's dreams," Beloît sang out. "Bless my stars—I'm in love."

Pierre stared in amazement as Beloît trotted over to a tall Ojibwe woman. In a jumbled mix of French and Ojibwe Beloît managed to ask her if she had a husband. When she finally shook her head, Beloît clapped his hands together and yelled, "It's my lucky day." Then he did a little dance in the sand.

"She's a bit broad in the beam for my taste," Augustine chuckled, "but the man sure is smitten."

By now Red Loon was smiling, and he turned to Pierre. "That's my widowed aunt," he explained.

"I'm sorry Beloît is so forward," Pierre replied, "but—"

"No need to apologize," Red Loon said. "Gasigens, or Little Cat as you would call her, hasn't smiled since her husband died last winter."

Pierre looked at Beloît. A group of women had now clustered around the bowman to get a closer look at his scarred face. They were pointing at his torn nose and whispering. Beloît was soon rolling his eyes back in his head and making silly faces that had them all giggling. *Je suis l'homme,*" he crowed.

Rat's Liver, who was clearly fascinated by Beloît's odd behavior, spoke to McHenry. "Your friend can scramble the cords of his face at will."

"That he can, sir," McHenry agreed. "That he can."

CHAPTER 11

Bastille Day

Since the next day was July 14, Bastille Day, McHenry declared a full day off in honor of the French national holiday. The men rested through the morning, smoking their pipes and telling stories. Shortly after midday, the commander told Bellegarde to tap a rum keg. The crew cheered, applauding McHenry for the clever way he'd turned events in his favor yesterday; then they began some serious celebrating.

Late in the afternoon Rat's Liver and his son paddled out to the island. "We should discuss a site for your post, William McHenry," Rat's Liver said. He eyed the cavorting crewmen with a slight smile.

"You'll have to excuse my men, but—" McHenry began.

"I know something of your customs."

While Rat's Liver retired to McHenry's tent, Red Loon visited with Pierre. Though Beloît stepped up and offered Red Loon a cup of rum, he politely shook his head.

"You don't know what you're missing, Loon Feather," Beloît said, returning to the rowdy bunch around the fire.

"My father forbids us to take liquor," Red Loon explained to Pierre. "As a young man he saw so many lives destroyed by strong drink that he won't allow it in our village. Though some of the men may sneak a dram—my uncle among them—nearly everyone supports the wisdom of his judgment."

"I can understand," Pierre said, nodding. Though Red Loon spoke slowly, his pronunciation was better than that of some of Pierre's classmates back home.

"So, what is this Bastille Day, as you call it?" Red Loon asked.

While the *voyageurs* slugged down their double rations of rum, Pierre tried to explain the history of the Bastille to Red Loon. "It was a huge prison in Paris," Pierre said. "Hundreds of men were locked up for no reason. The French Revolution began on the day the Bastille was stormed, and those men were freed."

Red Loon frowned. After he had asked a number of questions about what prisons were and where Paris was, he concluded that it was "silly to worry about such a faraway tribe."

At first Pierre laughed, but the more he thought about it, the more he had to agree. Life in the north was occupied with daily tasks like filling a berry basket or catching a trout. What had happened decades ago and thousands of miles away held no real importance. Like the ancient Greek Epicureans whom Sister had taught him about, the Ojibwe lived according to the philosophy *carpe diem,* or "seize the day." They relished the moment and didn't worry about tomorrow.

The next morning at dawn the men moved their camp to the mainland and began the job of clearing the land for their trading post. Rat's Liver had chosen a stand of red pine just above the sandy cove where the brigade first landed. The trees were straight and tall—ideal for cabin logs—and there was a dry, level building site. As a bonus, the beach offered a perfect landing for their canoes.

The men cut the underbrush and saplings first, tossing them onto a huge bonfire. While the older crewmen felled the pines, Louie and Pierre were given the dirty job of peeling off the bark. Working with two-handled draw knives from dawn to dark, the two boys spent the next week covered with pine sap.

Since they were working at the shaded edge of the clearing, mosquitoes pestered them until midmorning. With the coming of the sun, deerflies arrived to chew on them. And Pierre found that the pitch on his hands made it impossible to scratch his bites.

"I guess we just gotta let the bugs eat what they want of us," Louie said.

To make matters worse, a hot, humid spell settled in. From the moment Pierre picked up his draw knife in the morning until the time he was called for supper, a river of sweat trickled down his back.

"I feel like someone's poured swamp water down my pants," Louie said.

"Don't give Beloît any ideas."

One afternoon Pierre took off his cap during a pipe break, and it stuck fast to his sap-covered hand. As Pierre shook the cap loose, Beloît called, "What's the matter, pup, is your hat trying to bite you?"

The trading post was constructed with a system of notches and pegs. The men began by setting four grooved logs upright at the corners of the foundation. After the ends of the wall logs were shaped into splines, each one was slid into place. It was tricky and dangerous to roll the wall logs up makeshift ramps and slide them into place— Beloît was almost killed one afternoon when a rope broke and the butt end of a log nearly took his head off. Though the big logs were heavy to work with, the walls went up fast, since it took only six of them to make a seven-foot wall.

By quitting time, the sharp scent of pine had penetrated Pierre's skin, hair, and clothes. No matter how hard he scrubbed, there was no way to clean the amber goo off his body. Awake or asleep, the pungent odor of sap burned his nostrils.

At night the crew followed the same routine they had since they'd left Montréal last May. The men slept under the shelter of their canoes, while McHenry retired to his tent. Sometimes when Pierre woke late in the night, the commander's candle was still lit. Studying McHenry's thin silhouette framed against the tent wall, Pierre wondered what sort of reading or writing kept him up so late. But no matter how late the candle burned, McHenry rose early and never showed a hint of fatigue.

One evening after supper, Augustine told a story about a shipwreck he had survived in the Azores. When he was done, McHenry turned to Pierre. "Speaking of shipwrecks," he said. "Have you read *Robinson Crusoe*?"

"Yes, sir."

"Then let me show you something." The commander led Pierre to his tent. McHenry's journal lay open on a rough-hewn cedar plank that was supported by the two wooden book crates. Beside his journal was an inkwell and a quill pen. "I've been keeping a daily journal since 1789," he said. "I haven't missed a day in the last twelve years."

McHenry's library was lined up on two half-log shelves in the rear of the tent. The spines of the rich, leather-bound volumes were lettered in gold. Stepping up to the shelf, he said, "Here you are," and handed a slim brown volume to Pierre.

Pierre looked at the title, *The Life and Strange, Surprising Adventures of Robinson Crusoe,* and opened the book. "But this is written in English," he said. Assuming Mc-Henry had picked the wrong book, he handed it back to the commander. Though Pierre knew a little English, all his schoolwork had been in French or Latin.

"If you want to advance with the North West Company," McHenry said, "knowing a bit of English really helps. Nearly all the partners are British or Scots."

"I know—" Pierre stopped and stared at the book. "But how could I ever read a book this long?"

"You know the story, right?"

"Yes, but—"

"Have a seat then." McHenry motioned to a keg. "I'll get you started."

As the cabin building proceeded, Pierre noticed that the *voyageurs* did log work at the same frantic pace at which they portaged and paddled. "The harder we work," La Petite declared, "the sooner we sleep with a roof over our heads." Pierre was amazed at how quickly the buildings took shape. Once the walls were in place, the men cut spruce poles in a nearby swamp for rafters. Cedar bark finished off the roof, and the walls were chinked with a mix of mud and ashes. Though it was extra work, McHenry insisted on a puncheon floor, made of split logs pegged in place over the hard-packed dirt. A log chimney lined with clay, and oiled deerskin windows, gave the post a homey feeling.

The Ojibwe often visited the *voyageurs'* camp to watch, and Pierre got to know several of the men and boys. His favorite was Rat's Liver's son, Red Loon. Although Red Loon spoke only halting French, Pierre could understand him well enough, and Red Loon was anxious to practice.

If Ojibwe women stopped by camp, Beloît monopolized their company. They called him the One Who Makes His Face Dance and giggled loudly whenever he turned his eyelids inside out, made his eyes go round and round, or pulled his lip up over his nose. The other men were jealous when Beloît got all the attention, but they knew there was no competing with what André called his "rare idiot talent."

Each evening McHenry guided Pierre through the English version of *Robinson Crusoe*. Pierre faltered a lot at first, but as he read the book out loud, he soon discovered that many English words had Latin roots that he'd already learned in school. Before long, he was reading so well that McHenry could write in his journal and correct Pierre's occasional mistakes at the same time.

Beloît teased Pierre about his English lessons, saying "Where's your chalk and slate, schoolboy?" or "Too bad your mama isn't here to pack a lunch for you." But Pierre ignored him. Not only did he believe McHenry was right in stressing the importance of English, but he also loved Robinson Crusoe's story. Once Pierre got to the part where the shipwrecked sailor found a mysterious footprint in the sand, nothing could keep him from finishing the tale.

CHAPTER 12

Sweat Lodge

On July 31, 1801, the brigade celebrated the completion of its first building, a small log storehouse for trade goods. The *voyageurs* and Ojibwe gathered in front of the rough-hewn plank door while McHenry made a speech.

"I'd like to thank our Ojibwe friends for their generosity in sharing this rich land. . . ." As the commander spoke, Pierre noticed that Beloît, who was standing off to the side, had just loaded his North West gun with a double load of powder and was leaning a ladder against the gable end of the building. Then, winking at Pierre and putting his finger to his lips, Beloît climbed onto the roof.

Even though Pierre didn't say a word, in a short while everyone in the crowd was staring up at Beloît. "What in the blazes is going on?" McHenry said, stopping his speech and stepping back from the building to look for himself. When he saw Beloît he couldn't help grinning.

Beloît stood up and shouted, *"Vive Napoléon,"* discharging his musket at the same time. The kick of the gun tipped him backward, and when he went to plant a moccasin to steady himself, he slipped. Everyone's mouth dropped open as Beloît skidded out of sight down the back side of the roof.

Augustine was the first one to reach Beloît. "What a lucky fool," Augustine laughed. For Beloît had pitched headlong off the roof and landed in a pile of sawdust and wood chips, narrowly missing an ax and a chopping block.

Beloît looked up and mumbled, *"Je suis l'homme."*

The following Sunday, the only day of the week the *voyageurs* were free to do as they pleased, Red Loon approached Pierre. "My father asked if you would come to our sweat lodge."

"Sweat lodge?" Pierre repeated.

"The sweat lodge purifies us in both body and mind."

When they reached the edge of the village, a half dozen boys and girls were playing a game of hide-and-seek. One little girl was running in a circle. She was holding her nose and calling out, *"Me-e-mengwe, me-e-mengwe."*

"What's she doing?" Pierre asked.

"Calling butterflies." Red Loon laughed. "It may sound strange, but they really do seem to come."

The children ran up to Red Loon. The smallest girl tugged at his hand and asked him something. But he shook his head.

"What does she want?" Pierre asked, seeing the sadness in her dark eyes.

"It's nothing." Red Loon shrugged. "They want to play a silly game."

"I don't mind," Pierre said.

"Really?" Red Loon stopped. The small ones were already jumping up and down with joy.

Pierre nodded.

"Follow me," Red Loon said.

The two boys walked a short distance up the hill. Red Loon paused by a clump of hazel. He took out his knife and cut a handful of leafy branches, which he stuck all around his head band. All Pierre could see through the dark leaves were eyes and teeth.

Pierre chuckled. "Are you trying to disguise yourself as a tree?"

"Don't laugh." Red Loon smiled. "You're next."

"Oh, no," Pierre protested.

"Oh, yes," Red Loon insisted, cutting more branches and tying them around Pierre's head with a rawhide thong. Red Loon then picked up a stick and led Pierre to a cedar thicket. They crouched down in the shadows.

A moment later the Ojibwe children appeared, walking in single file and holding each other by the belt. They were peering cautiously from side to side. When they were less than ten paces away, Red Loon leaped to his feet, brandished the stick over his head, and let out a terrible shriek.

The children squealed and scattered in all directions. Red Loon ran after the little girl who'd been so anxious to play, picked her up in his arms, and pretended to bite her middle.

As she screamed and giggled, the other children ran back and pretended to hit Red Loon with sticks. Then Red Loon and Pierre chased the children, alternately attacking and retreating, and taking care not to scare the little ones too much.

After a while Red Loon declared that the game was over. "My father is waiting," he said. "But we will play again another day."

Red Loon brought Pierre to the far end of the village. Rat's Liver and an older man were kneeling over a fire. Behind them stood a blanket-covered framework of bent poles. They were heating round rocks on the coals. Red Loon said, "This is my uncle, Wawa'ckeci nonda' gotcigun."

Pierre's eyes widened. How could he ever remember such a name? Red Loon smiled and said, "His name means 'One Who Is Skilled at Calling Deer,' but you can just call him Uncle."

Rat's Liver and Wawa'ckeci both nodded to Pierre, but neither man spoke as they lifted three small stones with sticks and carried them into the lodge. When they returned for the largest stone, Red Loon's uncle said, "Be careful that the messenger does not fall."

When Pierre frowned, Red Loon said, "The big stone is called a messenger, because the steam that rises from it is sent to the spirit world." Then Red Loon motioned toward the lodge. "It is time." The men, who had already stripped to their breechclouts, stepped inside. Red Loon and Pierre took off their clothes and followed.

It was dark and warm in the lodge. The blanket-covered frame was no more than four feet in diameter, so the shoulders of the men nearly touched as they sat in a circle around the hot stones. Red Loon lit a pipe and drew in two deep puffs before passing it to his uncle, who did the same. Though Pierre didn't smoke, when his turn came he pulled politely on the pipe and was surprised to taste sweet willow bark instead of tobacco. The air was soon hot, and the lingering smoke clouded Pierre's eyes.

No one spoke until the pipe was returned to Rat's Liver. Then the chief dipped a bunch of grass into a water basin and sprinkled it on the largest stone. Beads of sweat gathered on Pierre's forehead as the steam rose. "Weeee . . . ho ho ho," Rat's Liver chanted, and the other men repeated a simple "Ho ho ho," three times, in a soft, musical rhythm.

When the chant was over, the grass was handed to the uncle, who sprinkled more water on the stone and spoke to it: "I wish that this messenger would ask the Mide Manido to bring us long and healthy lives." Then the chant was repeated.

As the grass and the water basin were handed to Pierre, he wondered what he might say. His head felt light, and his cheeks burned from the heat. What was proper? What might dishonor the occasion? He sprinkled the water on the stone and said simply, "May the fire never die." The words must have been fitting, for Rat's Liver and the uncle both nodded politely before they began the final chant.

After a moment of silence, Red Loon's uncle lifted the blanket from the doorway, and the men stepped outside. As they wiped the sweat from their faces and shared a drink of water, the uncle said, "Your friend speaks well, Red Loon. You must invite him to our wigwam this winter to share our stories."

Later, when Red Loon walked Pierre back to the post, he explained what his uncle had meant. "According to custom we only tell our legends when there is ice on the lakes and snow on the ground. It is a great honor to be invited. I'm sure your people have many fine legends that you can share with us."

That night as Pierre drifted off to sleep, he was wondering what sort of story he could possibly tell an Ojibwe chief and his brother. Cinderella? A Bible story like that of Noah's Ark? His eyes and throat still burned from the pipe smoke, but his body felt clean and light. Even the pine bark pitch had been loosened from his hands.

Something in the ceremony reminded him of the power he'd felt during his First Communion. Was it a sin, he wondered, to compare Father Michel's silver chalice to the sweet grass and smoke of the sweat lodge?

CHAPTER 13

Manitou

The Windigo Point Trading Post was completed in early October. Along with the storehouse, the men had built a cabin for Commander McHenry and a bunkhouse for themselves. Pierre was depressed the night McHenry left his tent for his new lodgings. Pierre had gotten used to the slender figure of the commander framed against the tent wall each evening. He and McHenry had talked a lot over the last few weeks. Would they visit as often now?

As soon as they had finished the last building, the commander invited Rat's Liver and his people over to celebrate. The *voyageurs* spitted two venison haunches over the white-hot coals of a big bonfire, and Bellegarde served liquor rations all around. Though the Ojibwe enjoyed the food, they politely refused the liquor, with the exception of Little Cat and Wawa′ckeci.

It wasn't long before Beloît got "rummed up" and made a perfect fool of himself. His weird face trick for the evening involved crossing his eyes and rotating them at the same time. The women were doubly amused when they saw that as Beloît drank more rum, his eyes were slower and slower to uncross.

Beloît invited Little Cat to dance, asking, "How about a spin, Kitten?"

Winking at Pierre, he whispered, "Dance 'em before you romance 'em, La Page. They can't resist a little lovin' after a quick whirl around the fire." Pierre blushed at this bad conduct, but Red Loon, who was standing next to Pierre, only laughed.

To make matters worse, as Beloît danced, he let out an occasional "Meow," which made Little Cat and the other Ojibwe women giggle. Though most of the *voyageurs* ignored his idiocy, Augustine was peeved.

"What's the use of me piping a tune with all your caterwauling, Jean Beloît?" he shouted.

"You make your music, Auggie, and I'll make mine." Beloît kicked his legs high and let out another screech.

One morning Red Loon stopped by the post and invited Pierre to go camping with him.

"I'll have to ask the commander," Pierre said, continu-

ing to work on the snowshoe frame he was fitting together.

After Red Loon watched Pierre work for a few more
minutes, he said, "Well, aren't you going to ask him?"

"How soon do you plan on going?"

"Today."

Pierre grinned. He was always amazed at how impul-
sive the Ojibwe were. They never worried about sched-
ules or planning.

When he asked permission, the commander said, "That
would be a good idea, son. It's wise to learn the lay of the
land before the trading season begins."

Pierre and Red Loon left later that morning. As they
hiked along the well-worn path that led off Windigo Point,
Pierre asked, "Would you have gone by yourself if I hadn't
been able to come"

"Of course," Red Loon said. "My father often chal-
lenges me to test my woods skills."

"Do you always travel this light?" Red Loon carried only
a small leather sack, his knife, and his bow. Pierre had a
pack on his back stuffed with his blanket and a few provi-
sions.

"Sometimes I travel with less. Last year my father
blackened my face and sent me into the woods for a week.
I fasted day and night, taking only a little water to keep up
my strength."

"But why?"

"Before a boy becomes a man, he must seek a dream.
Fasting lightens the mind so that it can see—"

Red Loon stopped suddenly. He raised his hand for silence.

Pierre stood for a long time before he heard anything. Then came a faint crashing followed by a grunting sound. Red Loon grinned and waved for Pierre to follow. They stalked up an aspen ridge, stepping only in the soft, mossy places where their moccasins would make no noise.

By the time they reached the top of the ridge, the noise was twice as loud. Kneeling in the shadow of a lone balsam, Red Loon pointed into the dark swale and whispered, "Look."

Pierre saw nothing, but the strange noise still continued. When he was ready to give up, he saw a dark patch of fur, then a head and an enormous rack of antlers. It was a bull moose!

If only I'd brought my rifle, he thought.

The huge beast was scraping his antlers on the brush, rubbing off strips of bloodred velvet that dangled from the rounded tips of his broad-fingered horns. After slashing the bark off a half dozen young aspen, the moose lowered his head and charged into a rotten old tree that was riddled with woodpecker holes. Pierre winced as the bull hit the tree with a loud crack. To Pierre's amazement, the tree shivered a moment and fell. A dust cloud rose from the dry leaves.

The moose shook his head from side to side and pawed the ground. Then suddenly he stopped.

"He's scented us," Red Loon said. "Watch this." With a grin he stood up and whistled.

Pierre's eyes went wide. What if the moose charged?

Then Red Loon waved his hand. Pierre looked for cover, but the moose gave a loud snort, wheeled, and plunged off into the brush. "They have great noses, but they don't see so well," Red Loon laughed. "He'll probably run all the way to Lost Lake."

"Lost Lake?" Pierre asked.

Red Loon nodded. He walked down the ridge and pointed across a huge swamp. "The lake's over there, a good two miles across the muskeg."

Pierre looked out at the vast tract of swamp. The moose was already small in the distance. "Look at him go," Pierre said.

When the boys turned to walk back up the ridge, Pierre paused to study the rotten tree the moose had knocked down. It was at least eight inches across, and it had cracked into three pieces when it fell. Pierre noticed a bright feather in the leaves. "Look at this," he said.

The feather was a soft russet color. It was about six inches long and had a dark band next to a splash of white on the tip. Pierre held it out to Red Loon.

"This is a strong sign," he said. "Perhaps it is your *manitou*. We will show it to my father when we return."

"Manitou?" Pierre asked, slipping the feather into his pack.

"Yes," Red Loon said with a nod, "a token for special protection." Pierre thought back to Beloît's story of the brave who'd had his throat slit for a gold nugget. Did he need such protection?

Pierre and Red Loon hiked west along the shore of Vermilion and made camp on a rocky ridge that overlooked the lake. "I call this sunset rock," Red Loon said. "My cousins and I have come here since we were small. The berry picking and the hunting are fine in these hills, and in that creek over there"—he pointed at a swampy inlet to the north—"we spear northerns this big in the spring." He spread his hands a yard apart and smiled.

For supper they walked down to the shore and caught two bass with a hand line. When Pierre drew out his knife to fillet the fish, Red Loon admired La Londe's carving on the handle, and Pierre told him about the day his old friend saved a canoe full of men.

Later, as the boys roasted their fish over an open fire, they laughed and joked as if they had known each other for a long time. At sunset Red Loon showed Pierre a broad white pine on the top of the ridge. The branches were smooth from the many moccasins that had climbed it. It reminded Pierre of an ancient oak near his home in Lachine that he and Celeste and his other friends often climbed. Father had tied two swings to a stout branch that pointed out toward the river. From that swing the children could watch the blue St. Lawrence and mark the arrival of the tall ships from the west and the canoe brigades from the east. Pierre wondered what Celeste was doing this evening, so far away. Were there quiet moments back in Lachine, when Celeste thought of him as he was thinking of her tonight?

"Let me show you the view." Red Loon grinned, catching a broad branch with both hands and swinging himself upward. A minute later the boys had climbed to a smooth-barked limb about twenty feet off the ground. "See that bay beyond the hill?" Red Loon asked. Standing up, he clenched the trunk with one hand and pointed to the west.

Pierre nodded. The air was heavy with the smell of pine, and a squirrel chattered noisily above their heads.

"From here we can see when the caribou herds are coming down from the north. The big water forces them to follow the shore, so they always cross somewhere close by."

"I didn't know there were caribou in this country," Pierre said.

"Some years they never get this far south. But when they do, the hunts are grand."

After the sun went down, the boys slept in the dried pine needles on top of the ridge. Though Pierre offered to share his blanket with Red Loon, the other boy shook his head. "My deerskin shirt is padding enough," he said. "That's why I wore it."

Though a few mosquitoes hummed close over Pierre's head when he first lay down, once the coolness of the full dark descended, the bugs disappeared. Pierre fell into a deep, dreamless sleep.

What seemed like only minutes later, he heard a half-human shriek. He froze, waiting for a creature to leap for his throat. When nothing happened, he sat up. Red Loon was already on his feet. His bow was at full draw, and he was aiming in the direction from which the horrible cry had come.

Pierre drew out his knife. His heart raced as he held his breath. In the moonlight Pierre could see the muscles in Red Loon's jaw tense as he stared into the shadows, trying to pick out a target for his arrow.

Suddenly there was a loud laugh in the darkness, behind them. When Red Loon turned, there was a second laugh on the opposite side. This time Red Loon chuckled too.

Pierre was confused until a voice boomed in the darkness. "You've done well, my son." Then Rat's Liver appeared.

After he had shaken Pierre's hand, Rat's Liver clapped his son on the back and said, "You've shown the readiness of a true warrior." He laughed. "Not like that time we tied your moccasins up, eh?"

Red Loon nodded. A moment later Red Loon's uncle appeared and also congratulated him. Then, before Pierre had fully awakened, they were both gone.

"What was all that about?" Pierre asked. His head throbbed with confusion. Had this all been a bad dream?

"I'm sorry," Red Loon said. "I should have warned you. The men of the village always test us like this. We must prove that we are ready for a Sioux attack. Sometimes the men give a war cry in the dark to see how fast we react.

Other times they sneak up and try to touch us with a coup stick.

"Once when I was very small," Red Loon continued with a smile, "I was camping with my older cousin, and my uncle crept up in the night and tied our moccasins together. He and his friends teased us for many days after. Though it is a game, it is a serious one, for men who sleep too soundly in the wild do not wake at all."

Pierre wanted to ask more questions, but Red Loon had already lain down and was snoring softly. How could he fall asleep so fast? It took Pierre many minutes to quiet the beating of his heart. Throughout the night he found himself waking at the smallest sound. Were the men still out there at the edge of the dark, creeping ever closer?

When the boys arrived back at the village the next morning, Rat's Liver greeted them with a huge grin. "Did you sleep well?"

After the joking was done, Red Loon showed his father the hawk's feather Pierre had found. Rat's Liver smiled. He took the feather and touched it to Pierre's head. "With such snowy hair, we must call you White Hawk. That will be your true name from this day forward." Then he stepped into his wigwam and came out with a small leather bag that was tied to a rawhide cord. "You must keep your *manitou* close to your heart." He put the hawk's feather in the bag and slid the cord over Pierre's head. Pierre fingered the soft leather pouch, feeling for a hint of magic in the ancient charm.

* * *

The next day Red Loon invited Pierre to go on a short trip with his father and uncle. "They want to inspect the wild rice crop that grows in the marsh at the end of the bay," Red Loon said. "We call the rice *manomin*."

"I know," Pierre nodded, remembering last summer's feast in Kennewah's wigwam.

"Then you know it is the most important food of my people."

Pierre nodded. Wild rice often saved the Ojibwe from starving when hard winters made game scarce.

Once again McHenry was pleased to let him go. "A poor rice crop," he said, "can mean trouble for us all."

Though they took Ojibwe canoes that morning, Pierre brought his own paddle. When he arrived at the beach, Red Loon's uncle pointed at him and cried, *"Ikweabwi!"*

Uncle took Pierre's short *voyageur* paddle from his hand. "*Ikweabwi* means 'woman's paddle,'" he said, standing Pierre's paddle beside his own. It was nearly twice as wide and long. "This one is man-sized."

While Red Loon went to get another paddle for Pierre, Uncle was still laughing. "Did you paddle so hard that you wore that one down?" he teased.

As soon as Pierre got into Red Loon's canoe, he could see the advantage of the Ojibwe paddle. By pulling slowly and deeply, he and Red Loon could propel this feather-light craft faster than a half dozen *voyageurs* could paddle a north canoe.

116

Skimming across the water in silence—there were no folk songs or sea chants for the Ojibwe—Pierre and Red Loon followed closely behind the lead canoe. When they arrived in a shallow bay a half hour later, Rat's Liver and his brother shipped their paddles. "Though we mainly harvest rice in a lake south of here," Red Loon said, "this small patch helps us judge the potential of the harvest."

Uncle reached for a stalk of wild rice and pulled the tufted head off. Then he crumpled the rice grains into his open palm. Repeating the process, he shook his head. When he finally spoke, his words sounded like a slow, sad song.

"It's worse than they thought," Red Loon explained to Pierre. "Low water makes for a poor crop, and that storm we had last week knocked off the small amount that was growing. It will be a meager harvest this year."

"But there's plenty of deer," Pierre said.

"For now there is plenty of everything, but the deep snows are soon to come."

CHAPTER 14

Denning up

The first heavy frost came in mid-September. At dawn, Beloît called Louie to the door. "Take a look, Half-pint," he said, swinging the split-log door open.

Still half asleep, Louie stared at a white world. "Snow?" he asked.

"It's a killing frost," Beloît said, "and the first blizzard ain't more than a spit and a grin behind."

Once the last of the buildings were finished, the daily routine at the post slowed considerably. The cold days they needed for preserving fish and game for the winter were still a few weeks away, and the pelts weren't yet prime for trapping. Stuck between summer and the trading season yet to come, the *voyageurs* spent their time doing simple jobs. They cut and chopped wood. They built furniture. They inspected the cedar bark roofs and the wall chinking of the cabins to make sure they were winter-tight. They made traps. They built frames and tied harnesses for the dogsleds that they would soon be running on trading trips.

The bright, cool days were a joy. Each day the hillside above the post brightened more and more from the changing leaves. With the mosquitoes and flies gone, Pierre and Red Loon and Louie enjoyed hunting squirrels and fishing and hiking along the maple ridge that ran to the end of the point. One day Red Loon showed the boys a crater that he claimed had been made by a falling star. Together they marveled at the huge hole and the blackened bits of rock around the edges, which looked as if they had been melted in an enormous oven.

But no matter how busy Pierre was, he missed home. Back in Lachine autumn was a time to help his father with the butchering and to help his mother and sisters gather apples. The previous fall when he'd returned from his first summer with the brigades, he and Celeste had taken long walks beyond the village.

"*Monsieur* Canoeman," she would tease, "are you sure you can travel so far without your paddle?"

"Not only do I not need a paddle, *mademoiselle,*" Pierre bragged, "but I could carry you from here to your father's doorstep."

"How bold we have become," she giggled.

Spending a whole year away from home would be more difficult than Pierre had imagined. When the brigade was on the move, he didn't have a chance to be lonesome. But time had suddenly slowed. These days his dreams were peopled by faraway places. The passing of Kennewah and her family haunted him. It was so unfair. Whenever he looked at the children playing in the Ojibwe village, he thought of Kennewah lying in a grave house above the dark waters of Lake Superior. Why her? Why them? Why . . . ? The questions rocked him to the core.

He was glad to be distracted by preparations for the trading season. McHenry and La Petite taught him how to keep the account book in which all the transactions were recorded. Using a system of pictures that showed which goods the company was advancing, they kept track of each family individually. McHenry praised Pierre's handwriting, but he teased him about the little symbols he drew. "What's this?" he said, staring at a picture of a leghold trap Pierre had drawn. "It looks like a set of false teeth."

"Well, how about my copper kettles?" Pierre asked.

"What do you think, La Petite?" McHenry said, showing him the tiny sketch.

"It looks like a milk pail to me," La Petite said, laughing.

McHenry and Pierre often sat outside the commander's door after supper and continued Pierre's English lessons.

Pierre had worked his way to the end of *Robinson Crusoe* and was already halfway through an English edition of Voltaire's *Candide*. One evening Pierre asked, "Did Voltaire make up the part of his book where nonbelievers are punished by being burned alive?"

"You're damned right they was burned, La Page," Beloît hollered from the bunkhouse door. "And the reason they was burned was they asked too many questions." Then, as he walked toward Little Cat's wigwam, he called over his shoulder, "Shouldn't school be out by this late in the day, ladies?"

"There's a fellow who's going to die as ignorant as the day he was born," Pierre muttered.

"Don't be too sure," McHenry said. "He knows more than he's willing to admit."

"Really?" Pierre asked.

As McHenry nodded, Pierre looked at the cackling fool. What could the commander possibly mean?

One day Louie and Bellegarde came back from a hunting trip and announced that they needed help dragging a big sow bear back to the post. Beloît and Pierre and Augustine all went along.

When they reached the carcass, Pierre was sad to see a bear cub bawling over its dead mother. It ran to the edge of the woods when the men approached, but it kept crying in the underbrush. As André and Augustine tied the front legs of the bear to a stout dragging pole, the cub walked right up to the mother and sniffed her. Then it bawled even more loudly.

André cocked his rifle, saying, "The kindest thing we can do is put it in the soup pot too."

Pierre turned his head, not wanting to see, but Beloît said, "Put down that gun."

"What?" André said.

"The little tyke deserves better than that."

Pierre couldn't believe his ears. The cruelest man he'd ever met was taking the side of a bear cub! "Come on, little fellow," Beloît added, taking a bit of venison jerky from his pouch. As the bear snatched the meat from his palm, Beloît said, "She sure is a runty one for this late in the year."

"How do you know it's a she?" Augustine asked.

"She's too cute to be anything but a little lady," Beloît said.

"A cub that small will never survive," André insisted. "Let's do the right thing."

But when André raised his gun again, Beloît spoke with his teeth clenched. "Put that thing away before I bend it around your ears."

André slowly lowered his gun.

The little bear bawled the whole way back to camp, alternately sniffing its dead mother and licking Beloît's hand as it begged for more food. "We'll get you something more when we get home," Beloît promised.

"Home?" André scoffed. "Why don't you stop babying that creature and help us drag this carcass?"

"Shut up," Beloît snapped. "Can't you see she's upset?"

As soon as they got back to the post, Beloît took some pork fat out of a keg and loaded it onto his tin dinner plate. "Here you go, girl."

He grinned proudly as the bear gobbled down every morsel.

When dinnertime came, Beloît could talk of nothing but his newfound friend. "Ain't she a cutie?" he declared as he stepped up to the dinner pot and held out his plate for André to load.

"Did you wash that off after the bear slobbered all over it?" Augustine asked from behind.

"Do you think I'm a pig?" Beloît said.

"We know you're a pig," André said, heaping his plate full.

Pierre gagged. Beloît hadn't wiped his plate off. Just when Beloît had done the grossest thing Pierre thought he possibly could, he did something worse.

As Beloît took a seat and pulled his spoon out, the little bear snuffled up beside him, stuck out her tongue, and lapped half the stew off his plate.

"Look at her." Beloît laughed proudly. "Now, that's bad manners. I got a perfect name for you—Marie Antoinette." The men, knowing the bad reputation of the recently executed French Queen, all chuckled.

But their laughter stopped when Beloît took a spoonful

off his bear-slobbered plate and shoveled it into his mouth.

"I knew it," Augustine moaned. "You are the most revolting pig of a man I've ever seen."

"I can't believe it," Louie groaned, and the rest of the men joined in.

Beloît said, "A fine stew, André," as he downed a second spoonful.

CHAPTER 15

Pluses and Minuses

As the hard maples turned to flaming red, and the birch and aspen and sugar maples slowly changed to burnished gold, the pace of life at the post quickened. Pierre was amazed at the amount of food André stored. He smoked venison jerky on wooden racks. He traded with the Ojibwe for dried berries, squash, maple sugar, and what wild rice they could spare. He set nets daily for whitefish and walleyes.

As the youngest crewmen, Pierre and Louie had to clean the fish. "Isn't this enough?" Louie protested one afternoon, as he gutted their twenty-fourth fish, slit its tail, and slid it onto the drying pole.

"We need at least three per day per man to make it through the winter," André insisted.

"But that's hundreds of fish!" Pierre said.

"We'll need lots of fuel to keep us going in the cold . . ." The cook paused and turned. "Stop that," he shouted.

Pierre laughed. Beloît's bear, Marie, had sneaked up to the drying pole and was tugging at a fish.

Yelling, "Get," at the top of his lungs, the cook picked up the nearest thing, which happened to be a fat white-fish, and threw it at the bear. The fish hit Marie in the side of the face, and she happily grabbed it in her teeth and dashed toward the woods. Pierre and Louie laughed as André screamed curses after her.

By now Marie Antoinette had become a fixture in camp, and Beloît didn't care how much the men teased him about his pet. He doted on Marie like a proud father, and the little bear followed him wherever he went. Once Beloît even tried coaxing Marie into going for a canoe ride, until McHenry put a stop to it. "We'll not risk damaging a boat to indulge your spoiled baby," he declared.

The Ojibwe were fascinated by Beloît's attachment to the bear, and they began calling Beloît Father Bear. At first Pierre assumed that the tribe was making fun of Beloît, but Red Loon told him the opposite. "The bear is a powerful spirit," he explained. "Your friend—"

"Don't call him my friend."

"Well," Red Loon began again, "he must have a special strength for the bear to choose him as her guardian."

"That bear just likes him because he feeds her," Pierre said.

"It is not that simple," Red Loon insisted.

And the more Pierre watched Beloît and Marie playing together, the more he had to admit that there was something special in their relationship. The bear brought out a softer side of Beloît—a side that Pierre had never seen in their two summers together.

An idea came to Beloît after supper one evening. The men had gorged themselves on their standard fall fare of venison and wild rice, and they had just settled back to light their pipes. Beloît was chattering at Marie, who had devoured her usual huge portion over André's usual protests, when Beloît stopped in midsentence.

"What's the matter?" La Petite asked. "Did your little lady friend finally talk back?"

"If she did," La Petite added, "I hope she told him to shut up." The men all laughed.

"She yawned," Beloît said.

"So would you if you sucked down that much food," André said.

"But don't you see what this means? It's fall," Beloît went on, not caring if anyone was listening. "It's time for little *mademoiselle* to take her winter's nap."

That said, Beloît took up a shovel and began digging at the far end of the encampment. The little bear waddled along behind him and sat sniffing at the piles of dirt Beloît piled by the hole.

"You digging for gold?" Louie called.

"Looks like he's starting a rose garden," Augustine said.

"Shut yer faces," Beloît yelled back. "I'm digging a house for my Marie."

The entire camp, McHenry included, burst into laughter, but Beloît refused to be dissuaded from his task.

Every night after supper for the next three days, he worked at hollowing out a deep hole for Marie. "You'll sleep pretty here," he said, pausing to scratch the little bear's ears.

When his house, as he called the angled hole, was finished, he tried to coax Marie into giving it a try. "Time to sleep," he declared, and led her toward the entrance. But she sniffed once at the dark edge and refused to venture inside.

Beloît tried everything. He tossed a bit of maple candy into the den. He crawled into the waist-deep hole himself and said, "Look at what a sweet little home I've dug for you." He even tried pushing the pudgy bear down the hole, but she planted her paws and wouldn't budge.

The whole camp roared. "Maybe she wants you to install a feather bed?" McHenry commented, and the men laughed even more loudly.

In a huff Beloît kicked a clump of dirt into the open hole and walked away.

A week later the little bear dug a hole of her own right

next to Beloît's excavation. After scraping some dried leaves into a pile at the entrance, she crawled inside and went to sleep. Though Beloît stood over the den and cursed the little bear for ignoring his "fine accommodations," Pierre could see that he was proud that Marie was clever enough to make her own winter shelter.

CHAPTER 16

Onabinigizis, or
Moon of the Crusted Snow

In mid-November, a warm spell caught the traders by surprise. The black skim of ice that had just covered the lake melted away, and for a week a hot breeze blew out of the south. Though André's smoked venison survived the heat, his fish all spoiled.

"It's dog food now," André announced after he visited the cache they'd made in the cedars to help keep the meat cool.

"You mean all that work went for nothing?" Louie said.

André nodded. Pierre thought back to the scales and slime the boys had washed off their hands, and the huge mounds of fish guts they'd buried in the garden.

"We've got to set those nets as soon as it cools back

down," André declared, "and hope we can manage a reasonable catch before the real cold hits."

The day they put out the nets again, the weather took a sudden turn for the worse. An icy wind howled out of the north, and in a single afternoon the temperature dropped forty-five degrees.

The next morning Pierre woke feeling as if something was wrong. He lay for a moment until he realized it was the quiet. He had never heard such perfect, unbroken stillness. After slipping on his moccasins, he opened the door. Ten inches of fresh snow had fallen during night, and more was coming down. The air had a damp, biting smell that stung his nose.

"Shut the door," La Petite groaned from his bunk. "Were you raised in a barn?" Pierre slipped on his woolen *capote* and, pulling the leather-hinged door shut behind him, stepped out into a world transformed.

Every detail of the landscape had been rounded and softened by the snow. The sharp lines of the benches and rooftops were lost. Pine branches that had been clusters of bright green needles the day before were now shapeless white clumps.

The snow signaled the official beginning of the trading season. The pelts would be prime now, and the snow would allow travel by dogsled. Traders and trappers alike could cover twice the distance they did on foot.

With the coming of the snows, Rat's Liver held true to his promise to share the tribal legends with Pierre. Red

131

Loon visited the post one morning and invited the *voyageurs* to attend a feast in his father's wigwam. Though Pierre was hoping that Beloît would not be included, Red Loon said Little Cat insisted that a special invitation be extended to Brave Bear, as she called him.

The delicious meal reminded him of the summer when he and La Londe had dined with Mukwa at Grand Portage. Red Loon's mother served smoked whitefish, duck boiled with wild rice, fire-baked squash, and fried bread. For dessert she offered roasted hazelnuts and maple candy, followed by bowls of wintergreen tea.

As he sat in the tight circle of men, Pierre thought of Kennewah. How unfair it was that he should be feasting on fine food and drinking sweet tea while she slept in the cold company of the grave house. He recalled, as he had a hundred times, the soft, straight-parted hair that glistened in the firelight, the white doeskin dress, the shy smile. What justice could there be in taking such beauty from the world?

After the meal, Rat's Liver said, "Now that the earth is covered with snow and the lake is sleeping under ice, the time has come when we may share the strength of our legends with you."

"There's nothing like a good yarn to pass a winter's night," Beloît declared. Pierre was embarrassed, but Rat's Liver only smiled politely.

The story the chief told involved three men who went on a quest to meet Winibojo, the Master of Life. Each of the men hoped Winibojo, a famous trickster, would use his great powers to grant him a wish.

"After journeying for many days and enduring many hardships," Rat's Liver said, "the men finally arrived at the wigwam of Winibojo. Thinking that the great master would be quick to grant their requests, the boldest of the men stepped forward and said, 'Great one, I ask that you may give me the gift of eternal life.'

"In scorn Winibojo picked up the man and threw him into the corner, where he was turned into a black stone. 'Now you will last as long as the earth,' he declared.

"The second spoke with more care. 'Noble Winibojo, lord of all the universe, I ask that you give me the gift of wisdom and cleverness.'

" 'Be it so,' " said Winibojo, and with a wave of his hand he turned the man into a crow that flapped away, cawing in the dry wind.

"The last man, knowing that he must put all hope of personal gain aside, said, 'I humbly ask that you give me the power to heal my people.'

"Winibojo leaped up from his seat. The man trembled. But then the Lord of All Things smiled and handed him a medicine bag and a beautiful red sash. 'Take these,' he said, 'and be forever blessed.'

" 'And as a further reward I offer my daughter's hand in marriage, so that the happiness you bring to others will also be multiplied unto yourself.' "

"Ha, Ha." Beloît winked broadly at Little Cat.

The chief concluded with a quiet nod and said, "Now perhaps one of our friends might share a tale of their people."

Beloît poked Pierre in the ribs, shouting, "How about La Page here—he's a dictionary-head if there ever was one. Tell us all a story, Pierre."

Pierre blushed. Why doesn't this fool ever keep his mouth shut? he wondered. Everyone turned toward Pierre and waited. He searched his mind for a myth or legend that might fit the moment. He could think of nothing that would compare with Rat's Liver's poetic tale.

"What's the matter, La Page?" Beloît said. "Is your head so jumbled with schoolbook nonsense that you can't talk?"

Pierre began slowly, still having no idea which story he would tell. "I remember an ancient tale that Sister told our class one day." He paused.

He sought to reconstruct a Greek myth in his mind. "This tale, too, is about the power of wishes. It begins in a small stone hut in a faraway country called Greece, many, many years ago. There was an old farmer named Baucis, who had been married to his good wife, Philemon, for fifty-five years. Though they had very little money, they lived good and holy lives." Beloît rolled his eyes and yawned.

"One day the god of all gods, Zeus, came down to visit the town where this couple lived. Disguised as a beggar, he went from home to home, asking for the small favor of food and lodging. He approached the wealthiest homes in the town, but the merchants and bankers, the politicians and priests, all turned him away."

Beloît laughed and nodded. "That'd be just like rich folks."

"As night drew near," Pierre continued, "Zeus reached the poor farm of the old couple, Baucis and Philemon. The great god, though he was dressed in tattered rags, received a warm greeting. 'You look weary, stranger,' Baucis said. "You are welcome to a place by our fire, and a share of our modest supper.'

" 'Thank you, good sir,' Zeus said. Philemon then offered the visitor a small bit of bread and cheese—all that they had in their larder—and invited him to spend the night. When Baucis and Philemon both apologized for their poor accommodations, Zeus said, 'You have offered me all that you have. What more could a guest ask?'

"The next morning Zeus revealed his true identity. 'Though I plan on punishing your fellow villagers with a thunderbolt when I return to Mount Olympus,' Zeus declared, 'for your hospitality, old ones, I will grant whatever wish you request.'

"Baucis touched his wife's hand and smiled. 'Thank you for your generous offer,' he said. 'But we have everything we could ever want in this world—food and shelter, love, and the freedom to pray.'

"Zeus was amazed. 'But surely there must be some small thing you could use—a palace, a bag of gold or jewels?'

"Philemon then whispered something to Baucis, and he smiled. 'Perhaps—' Baucis began.

" 'Go on,' Zeus prompted him.

"The wish the old couple made was that neither one of them should die before the other. 'If you could spare us, Great One,' Baucis asked, 'the agony of ever having to live alone, we would be forever grateful.'

" 'It shall be done,' Zeus replied, shaking his head in wonder at the holiness he had found in this small stone hut.

"A quarter of a century later the god's promise came true. It was a fine autumn day, and Baucis and Philemon had just celebrated their hundred first birthdays. They were walking their slow but steady way home through an olive orchard, when they paused to admire the setting sun. As they clasped hands and their faces set in satisfied smiles, a wondrous transformation took place. There was a clap of thunder high up in the pale sky. The ground trembled, and a cloud of smoke settled over the orchard. When the air cleared a few minutes later, Baucis and Philemon were no longer people, but two young olive trees, growing side by side, their roots and branches forever entwined."

Pierre glanced at Beloît, expecting a sneer, but he was surprised to see him squeeze Little Cat's hand and whisper something into her ear.

CHAPTER 17

Making Ice

Deep winter days soon descended on the trading post. The temperature dropped to ten or twenty below zero each night, and the lake boomed like a fusillade of cannons as the ice thickened. Sometimes the rumbling and cracking was so loud that Pierre had trouble falling asleep. To Pierre's amazement, an ice pressure ridge in the middle of the bay piled up to the height of a man. "Those are tricky places," La Petite warned. "There'll be open water behind that ridge no matter how cold the weather turns."

Though the thought of crossing open water in winter worried Pierre, he got his worst scare in his own bunk. After a long day of splitting and piling firewood, he was sleeping deeply one night when the sound of a pistol shot

137

awoke him. He let out a yell and sat up. The wall behind him was still echoing as he rapped his head on the bunk above him and moaned in pain.

Beloît roared with laughter as Pierre rubbed his aching head. Pierre was confused. No one carried a gun. There was no powder smoke in the room either. "What on earth was that?" he groaned.

"The logs," La Petite replied. "Go back to bed."

"The logs?"

"That's what I said," La Petite mumbled. Beloît was laughing so hard that it was difficult to hear the big man's sleepy voice. "When the green ones dry out, they crack sometimes. Especially on cold nights like this."

"That loud?"

"That loud. Go back to sleep."

As Pierre lay back, he wondered at the enormous power that had just shivered through the wall above his head. He waited for another crack, but nothing came. He finally drifted back to sleep.

With the coming of the snow, the pace of work at the post accelerated. Indian trappers regularly brought prime pelts from the neighboring villages of Wakem-up and Nett Lake, and the *voyageurs* traveled by dogsled to trade with bands as far west as Pokegama and Big Sandy lakes.

The winter jobs showed Pierre new sides of his crew. André was supposed to be the dogsled expert, and he promised to teach Pierre and Louie how to harness and run the dog team. But the boys soon discovered that he spent more time cursing the dogs than training them. He claimed that the dogs McHenry bought from the village were "unteachable" because they only understood "Indian talk." When a dog was lazy he'd yell *"Sacré chien mort"* ("Damned dead dog") and crack his whip in the frosty air. The dogs yelped at the sound of the rawhide snapping over their heads, but they never pulled any faster than half-speed for the cook.

However, whenever McHenry or La Petite took charge of the team, a simple *"Marche"* got the dogs running full speed ahead.

The *voyageurs* ran their dog teams with the same pride they took in racing their canoes. Much teasing was dished out to the team that couldn't keep up when two men were on the same trail. A slow sled was said to be "planted," and to escape that humiliation a man would push his five-hundred-pound sled along so that his dogs would not get too far behind. Fatigue and frostbite were small pains compared to ridicule. Anyone who tried to get sympathy by complaining was dismissed with "Wipe your own tears."

While André fought with his dogs, Augustine spent most of his winter days making furniture. Skilled in wood-working from what he called "whittling away the idle time aboard ship," Auggie showed himself to be a true crafts-man. Working with just an ax, a draw knife, and a rusty file that he bent and tempered in the fire, the old sailor made everything the men needed: tables, chairs, snowshoe frames, benches, sled runners, spoons, and bowls.

One afternoon after he'd carved a particularly fine bowl out of a swirly-grained block of maple, he held it up with pride. "There's a shape hidden in every piece of wood, mate," he said to Pierre. "The trick is to let it surface on its own." The scent of fresh maple lingered in the air, and Auggie was smiling in the soft light that filtered through the deerskin window. "It's a lot like loving a woman . . ." Augustine paused and whispered a name.

Pierre knew something of how the old sailor felt. A sudden loss—like the death of Kennewah's family—cut quick and deep. It left you hanging. Pierre wanted to know more about Augustine's life, but the sailor quickly changed the subject. "Would you look at that?" he said, holding his index finger up to the light. There was a spot of blood. "I've gone and cut myself."

During the winter the Ojibwe village was just as busy as the trading post. While Red Loon and the older boys went out trapping with the men, the younger children played in the snow. They raced each other on snowshoes. They "snow coasted" down the hill above the village on slender lengths of wood. They had contests throwing hooked sticks called "snow snakes."

On Sundays Pierre would often walk to the village and watch the Ojibwe children at their games. One day Red

Loon showed Pierre how to throw the curved snow snake so that it cut deep under a snowdrift and popped up on the far side. "When the snow is packed hard in the spring," Red Loon said, "we see how far we can skip these sticks across the top of the snow. A good throw goes farther than a strong man can shoot a bow."

Just then Beloît and Little Cat came by. They paused to watch the children skiing down the hill on curved bark slats that were only four inches wide. Beloît poked Little Cat in the ribs and said, "How about if I give it a try?"

Giggling as always, she agreed.

The children gathered on the hillside to watch Father Bear make his first run. When a little boy offered Beloît a balancing pole to steady himself, Beloît brushed it aside. "I don't want nothing slowin' me down," he declared.

Along with his woolen *capote,* Beloît wore summer leggings that left his thighs exposed to the cold. Pierre and most of the other men wore deerskin pants, but Beloît called them cowards. Pierre shivered as he watched the bare-legged bowman place one big moccasin on the ski and push off with his free foot. *"Je suis l'homme,"* he yelled.

Pierre's eyes widened as the husky man hurtled down the hill. The track was icy from the many skis that had gone before him, and Beloît's extra weight made him fly twice as fast as any of the children had.

Red Loon asked, "Will he know enough to sit down?"

With his arms wheeling wildly and his free foot dancing on the snow, Beloît bellowed the whole way down the hill.

As he shot onto the flat above the village, Little Cat called, "Stop, Jean Beloît. Stop, my darling."

Beloît was still traveling at top speed when he hit the first wigwam. Sheets of birch bark, bent poles, and blankets flew into the air as the shelter exploded. A yelping dog leaped out of the doorway, barely escaping with his life. Beloît never came out of the second wigwam. Little Cat found him lying dazed beside the smoldering fire pit. "My Beloît," she called, falling to her knees.

By the time Pierre and Red Loon and the curious children arrived, Beloît was already on his feet. Though he was tipsy, he refused help. "Tell the lady of the house that I'll help put her wigwam back together," he told Little Cat, spitting a loose tooth from his mouth into ash-stained snow.

CHAPTER 18

Holiday Bride

On Christmas Eve, McHenry invited Rat's Liver and his people to the post for a celebration. Two dozen Ojibwe, along with their children and babies, crowded into the bunkhouse with the *voyageurs* on the evening of the party. As a young mother leaned her cradle board against the wall and kneeled to check on her baby, Pierre recalled the gentle way Kennewah had tended to her brother Kewatin last summer. It was haunting to remember the little fellow's innocent smile.

The smells of roast venison, beaver tail stew, and steamed wild rice mingled with the earthy scents of wood smoke, oiled moccasins, and wet blankets. The Ojibwe brought two drums and a wood flute to add their music to Augustine's pipe. The men took turns playing songs at

143

first, but by the time the stew pot was bubbling in the fireplace, they'd formed an impromptu band and were playing a lively mix of native songs, jigs, reels, and folk tunes.

With the exception of Red Loon's uncle and Little Cat, the Ojibwe refused the rum. Not caring if they drank alone, the *voyageurs* toasted each other freely. And with every dram the noise in the room increased.

The energy was a shock to Pierre. He was used to the quiet hymns and candlelight of Christmas services back in Lachine. Though Father Michel smiled more broadly than usual on Christmas Eve, his conduct remained formal. Last year Pierre had spent more time studying Celeste than listening to Father's words. He recalled the moment she had stood for the benediction in her family pew at the head of the church. Her white shawl and bonnet had heightened the sparkling gold of her ringlets, as light danced off the frosty windows and filled the balsam-scented air.

As the *voyageurs* got wilder, the Ojibwe men and women paused in their dancing to stare. They were amazed at how fast the traders transformed themselves into stumbling fools.

But of all the stumbling fools, Beloît was the most obnoxious. "Let's hear that pipe, you weak-lunged landlubber," he bellowed at Auggie as he spun Little Cat in a tight circle and then lifted her high in the air.

"Whew," he whispered at Pierre, "this one's more work than a triple-packed load on an uphill portage." Turning to Little Cat, he added, "Ain't you, honey pot?" and kissed her plump cheek.

Beloît was dancing so wildly that Pierre was afraid he was going to hurt someone. In fact, in the middle of a crazy leaping jig, he accidentally kicked André in the seat of his pants and sent him flying across the room. At first it looked as if there would be a fight, but when André made a grab for the bowman, he tripped over a baby in a cradle board and stumbled into the wall. The angry mother stomped toward André, shaking a finger in his face. Just before a fierce three-way battle began, Beloît settled it all by hugging both injured parties and persuading them to dance with each other.

Pierre was surprised when McHenry joined in the fun. After opening his private stock of sherry and sharing it with the men, he even tried his hand at dancing.

"Mademoiselle," he said, bowing elegantly to a pretty girl named Gageanakwad, or Clear Sky, who was Rat's Liver's eldest daughter, "would you care to take a turn?"

The men grinned as McHenry, oblivious of the confusion around him, offered his arm to Clear Sky. The commander then led the beautiful girl through the intricate steps of a fancy ballroom dance.

As the couple weaved gracefully around the crowded room, Rat's Liver beamed proudly. Later, when McHenry and Clear Sky retired to McHenry's quarters, Rat's Liver

145

slapped Pierre on the shoulder and declared, "That's as fine a match as I ever could have hoped for."

Pierre frowned. It was hard for him to believe that Rat's Liver was so accepting of his daughter's relationship. But the next morning he understood.

Pierre awoke to the sound of heavy snoring. The men were sleeping off the effects of their party. Pierre shivered. The bunkhouse was so cold that he could see his breath, and when he tried to lift his head, he was shocked to discover that his hair was frozen to the outside wall.

Pulling his stiff hair gently from the logs, he looked around. Overnight the bunkhouse had been transformed into a crystal palace. Moisture from the steaming platters of food and the frantic dancers had crystallized on every surface. Everything from the tables and chairs to the log tie beams and the ceiling was diamond flecked. Tiny rainbows glittered in the light from the windows.

As pretty as it was, Pierre was too cold to admire the scene for long. He needed to start a fire. He stepped outside to get some wood. The morning was blue and still. He smiled as he passed McHenry's cabin on his way to the woodpile. If he hadn't seen the commander's stylish dancing last night, he never would have believed it.

Pierre loaded his arms with wood. When he returned, the door of McHenry's cabin was partly open, and the commander stood there talking in a louder-than-normal voice. "I'd like to thank you for your company," he said, "but I'm sure you'll be wanting to get back to your family. Your father must be expecting you"—he pointed toward the village—"at home." McHenry nearly shouted the word *home* but stopped suddenly when he saw Pierre.

"Ah . . . g-good morning, La Page," he stammered in embarrassment. Clear Sky waved to Pierre from inside. "I was just trying to explain to Clear Sky that—"

"William McHenry," a voice boomed across the yard, "I knew I'd find you up."

Pierre turned. It was Rat's Liver. He had a blanket across his shoulders, but his head was bare. He was grinning hugely.

"Hello, Rat's Liver," McHenry answered. "I'm so glad you've come. There's been a terrible misunderstanding. Though I've explained to Clear Sky that she's free to go home, either my Ojibwe is so poor or her French is—"

"Her French is very good," Rat's Liver said. "Though she can't speak it very well, she understands nearly everything she hears. For certain she knows about marriage *à la façon du pays*." That meant "according to the custom of the country."

"But—" McHenry stopped.

"I am honored, William McHenry," Rat's Liver declared, "to welcome you into my family."

"Really, Chief." McHenry tried one last time. "There's been a misunderstanding."

Rat's Liver only smiled and extended his arms to embrace McHenry. "From this day forward you are my son."

CHAPTER 19

Stalking the Long Shadows

The coldest weather of the season began the day after New Year's, when McHenry's thermometer registered what he estimated to be fifty degrees below zero. The cold was so bitter that even the toughest *voyageurs* stayed close to the fire, unless they needed to carry firewood or haul water.

One morning when Little Cat and Clear Sky were helping André serve breakfast, Beloît teased McHenry about his new wife. "It's sure nice to have a bunkmate to warm your bones in weather like this, eh, Commander?" he chuckled, giving Little Cat a squeeze.

Pierre blushed. McHenry looked ready to chastise Beloît. He pushed his bowl aside and touched his index finger to his temple, as if the bowman were giving him a headache, but then he smiled at Clear Sky.

"You're absolutely right, Jean," he said. Clear Sky was smiling now too. "Had I met a lovely lady like this two decades ago, it would have spared me many a lonely night on the frontier." Pierre knew that McHenry really cared for Clear Sky, and he was proud that he would admit it in public.

"Ain't that the truth," Beloît laughed. "I've never spent a winter in the north without a wife, and as long as I got my health and my good looks, I don't intend to."

His comment about good looks brought up a chorus of boos from the table. Augustine declared, "If it was good looks you were depending on, you'd have to shop for your wives at an almshouse for the blind."

When Pierre and Louie stepped outside to get an armload of firewood after breakfast, Pierre was startled by the bone-numbing cold. An instant chill penetrated his heavy woolen *capote* and cap and made him shiver. He sucked in a deep breath. His lungs burned, and as he exhaled, his eyebrows and eyelashes frosted over. Though it had been cold before Christmas, Pierre had never experienced anything like this.

On the way to the woodpile, the boys' moccasins squeaked so loudly on the packed snow that they both laughed. He and Louie took turns starting and stopping, shifting their feet and grinning at the weird sounds. "It's as if the ground is in pain," Louie said.

Pierre nodded. "You should see the steam coming off your head." He looked at the top of Louie's red wool cap. It was already turning white with frost, and a vapor trail was rising off his head and shoulders.

"You should see yourself," Louie said.

Feeling the bright cold creeping down his neck, Pierre said, "Let's get moving." With their shoulders hunched forward, they hurried toward the woodpile.

As Pierre bent to gather an armload of split birch, he saw that a small icicle was already hanging from Louie's nose. "Your nose has grown, *monsieur*." Pierre laughed so hard that he dropped a stick of firewood.

"Be careful of who you criticize," Louie replied, pointing toward Pierre's face. Sheepishly Pierre wiped the back of his mitt across his nose. The leather felt like tree bark against his skin.

The low was "only" twenty-five below the following night, and for the next two weeks the thermometer, even at midday, never rose above zero. The skies stayed clear and blue, but the sun had little power. The smoke from the chimney tops dipped toward the ground, instead of rising, and trailed off in a thin, white cloud across the frozen lake.

To make matters worse, during the middle of the cold spell, Beloît had an accident with the bunkhouse door. Anxious to get to the outhouse one morning before dawn, he nudged the door with his shoulder. The leather hinges cracked in half, and the door fell into a snowbank. The men inside woke to a frigid blast of wind. Cursing both

Beloît and the cold, Augustine and André leaped up from their beds to prop the door back in place. Though the final repairs were made during the warmest part of the day, it still took two hours of a roaring fire to warm the bunkhouse to above freezing.

When Pierre stepped outside at night, the stars were bigger and brighter than anything he'd ever seen. Despite the cold, he often paused to study the constellation Orion. He could imagine how ancient peoples must have stared into this same black sky and admired the bright-belted hunter.

When the cold spell finally broke, deep snows came. The first day the temperature rose above zero, a foot of fresh snow fell. And it kept on coming. Some days it was only a light dusting; other days six or eight inches fell. By week's end there were four feet of new snow. This, added to the two feet that had fallen before Christmas, made the woods difficult for travel. The snow was so light and powdery that men on snowshoes sank to their knees.

Since the post was short of meat, McHenry dispatched hunting parties every day, but neither the Ojibwe nor the *voyageurs* came home with anything larger than a rabbit or a spruce hen.

One day Pierre's group returned with only three squirrels after an entire day in the woods. Over supper that night every man had his own explanation for the poor hunting. One blamed the full moon; another said it was bad luck; but La Petite's made the most sense: "The deep snows and the cold drive the game south."

La Petite's logic didn't stop the complaining. The men had been grumbling over their meager portions of wild rice for two weeks. An occasional rabbit or squirrel did little to ease their hunger for fresh meat. André hooked a few fish on a hand line through the ice, but the deep snow and the three-foot-thick ice made fishing nearly impossible.

"How can a man fill his belly on this?" Louie whined over his plateful of rice.

"Be thankful we still got rice," La Petite replied. "I've seen men so hungry that they chewed the leather off their pack straps and was glad to have it."

When Louie looked at him doubtfully, the big man went on. "Anything is edible if you boil it long enough. Why, if you got a pinch of salt even a scrap of rawhide lacing or a moccasin top will do just fine. Ain't that right, Commander?"

The men turned toward McHenry. Though McHenry rarely spoke about his past exploits, everyone paid close attention whenever he told a story.

McHenry grinned at La Petite's tale. "It does get rough out there sometimes," he admitted. "I remember the first winter I spent on the Arctic Barrens. Traveling with the Chipewayan Indians, I ate the same things they did. If you get hungry enough, deer entrails, buffalo brains, and beaver fetuses are all palatable."

"Maybe this rice isn't so bad after all," Louie said, and the men laughed.

"But my favorite dish," McHenry continued, "was a lot

like the haggis that the Scots cook in a sheep's stomach. It was half-chewed caribou meat, boiled in the animal's stomach and smoked over a fire. Though it sounds awful, I acquired a real taste for that stuff. About the only thing I couldn't tolerate was eating raw bugs. Those Chipeway-ans used to gobble down warble flies and lice like Christmas candy."

Louie turned pale at the mention of boiled caribou stomach, and even Beloît, who prided himself on what he called his cast-iron guts, frowned at the thought of eating raw insects. "I'd sooner . . . ," he began, searching for a fitting comparison.

"Sooner take a bath?" Augustine offered.

But Beloît shook his head. "I wouldn't go that far," he said, and the whole company chuckled again.

The *voyageurs* were so desperate for meat that Mc-Henry sent the entire brigade out in pairs to scout for game. "The deer have got to be yarded up somewhere, now that the snow's so deep," he said. "Look for cedar thickets, spruce swamps—anywhere there's browse and protection from the weather."

Since the Ojibwe were hunting too, Red Loon and Pierre volunteered to go together. The next morning at dawn Red Loon invited Pierre to a ceremony in the woods near his wigwam. The local *midewin,* or medicine man, Odinigun, was on hand to bless their hunt. The men of the village began by blackening their faces with ashes and singing songs. Then Odinigun put sweet grass and medicine on the fire and waved the smoke over the hunters' clothing and guns. Finally the *midewin* dipped his hand in red paint and touched the shoulder of each warrior.

Pierre and Red Loon put on their snowshoes and shouldered their muskets, shot bags, and powder horns. As they started up the packed trail, Pierre asked, "What do the ashes mean?"

"The men have vowed that they will eat no more until we've found game. If the luck of our hunters doesn't change soon, our children will go hungry. They probably would have starved already if it wasn't for the pemmican that my father traded for."

"Pemmican?" Pierre asked, recalling the mix of berries and buffalo fat that was a staple of the tribes further west.

Red Loon nodded. "He traded McHenry's coat for two big bags."

Though the *voyageurs* were running short of food, it was clearly worse for the Ojibwe, who had many small children to worry about. Pierre admired Rat's Liver's generosity in giving up his elegant blue coat.

The boys silently followed the main trail. Since the snow had been packed down by the many hunters, the walking was easy at first. Two miles from the village freshly broken trails branched east and west along the shore of the lake.

Pierre and Red Loon paused to study the two routes. "How about that ridge?" Pierre asked, waving his arm toward a pine stand further west.

Red Loon didn't answer. He was facing due south,

studying a barren patch of tamaracks. Pierre frowned. "There won't be any deer out there."

With a slight smile Red Loon turned. "Who says we have to hunt for deer?"

"What else would we . . ." Pierre stopped speaking, recalling the bull moose they'd sighted near the Lost Lake Swamp during the fall. The hawk's feather he'd found that day still hung in a pouch from his neck. "You're not thinking of going after moose?"

"If we want to fill the cooking pot," Red Loon said, "why waste our time on small game?"

"We can't do any worse than the fellows who've been bringing in squirrels." Pierre grinned at Red Loon. "Lead the way."

An hour later Pierre regretted his words. The drifts were waist-deep, and their snowshoes tipped sideways. Though they took turns breaking the trail, by the time they had crossed the swamp they were both exhausted.

The temperature was bitterly cold, but Pierre was sweating so heavily that he pulled off his woolen *capote* and tied it around his waist. Red Loon opened the laces of his heavy deerskin shirt. As the steam rose off their shoulders, Red Loon joked, "We look as if we're ready to leap from a sweat lodge into the snow."

"Or as if . . ." Pierre stopped in midsentence when Red Loon suddenly raised his hand.

Pierre heard the sound too. Both boys raised their guns. The loud crackling of the brush was a sure sign a moose was nearby. Though deer tended to be silent in the woods, moose often charged straight ahead, trampling everything in their path.

A moment later the sound began to fade. Red Loon cursed and uncocked his gun.

"We must've jumped him," Pierre said.

Red Loon nodded. "I'll bet he was bedded just ahead."

Only a hundred yards into the woods, the boys found a melted spot at the base of a balsam where the moose had been lying down. Pierre whistled softly when he saw the size of the bed and said, "He must be huge."

"Maybe it's that big bull we saw last fall?"

Fresh tracks led up the hillside. A deep trough between the hoofprints showed where the belly of the animal had dragged in the snow. In a brushy opening a little further on, older tracks crossed the lowland in all directions. As far as the boys could see, the brush had been browsed off chest-high. "The moose have been eating breakfast, lunch, and dinner here," Pierre said, staring at the bushes that looked as if they'd been pruned flat by a gardener.

Red Loon nodded, silently studying the slope of the hill. "He was downwind of us," he concluded. "I'll bet he circles around. If we head back the way we came, we might cut him off."

"Let's go!"

The boys hustled to a low swale, where they paused to catch their breaths. Red Loon pointed his musket toward a ridge to the west, saying, "That looks as good as any place." Red Loon's blackened face was streaked with rivulets of sweat, and it gave him a wild look.

"You're leaking," Pierre said.

Red Loon frowned and repeated *leaking* as if he might be misunderstanding the French, so Pierre pointed to his chin.

Red Loon touched his face and smiled when he saw his ash-stained finger. "I hope I don't scare him away."

Keeping the wind in their faces, the boys sneaked up a pine ridge. When they found a place that gave them a clear view of the opening below, Red Loon whispered, "Let's wait here."

A half hour passed. Though Pierre pulled his *capote* back on, he was chilled to the bone. His feet went from aching cold to numb. Just when he was ready to suggest they try somewhere else, he heard the familiar crackling. Red Loon raised his hand to make sure his friend had heard. Pierre nodded.

A few minutes later, the moose appeared. Huge and black, it was browsing casually, biting off the tops of the alder and chewing as it walked. If it wasn't the giant bull they'd seen last fall, it was his twin. Weaving back and forth through the brush, the moose drew ever closer to the boys. Pierre held his breath, hoping the wind wouldn't change and give them away.

Just before the animal walked within range of their guns, he stopped. With his head down, he kept eating, casually flicking his comically big ears.

Pierre was just getting ready to draw back the hammer on his gun when the moose lay down. "A nap?" Pierre whispered. He couldn't believe his eyes.

After a long while both boys were shivering with cold. Red Loon whispered to Pierre, "We have to risk a stalk."

Thinking of the hungry children back at the Ojibwe camp, Pierre agreed. Both boys cocked their guns and started slowly down the hillside. Keeping a big white pine between them and the moose, they crept forward. Once the moose lifted his head to sniff the air, and they froze.

When they finally got to the pine, Red Loon motioned for Pierre to creep around the left side of the tree while he went to the right. As both boys stepped into the open, Red Loon whispered, "Now."

It was a difficult shot, but Pierre aimed for the shoulder and squeezed. At the same instant a smoke plume issued from Red Loon's gun. The moose crashed into the snow.

The boys cheered. Red Loon jumped up to celebrate, but the toe of his snowshoe hooked on a buried branch, catapulting him into a snowbank. Pierre roared with laughter. Red Loon, his face smeared with snow and ashes, laughed too. When he tried to stand, his snowshoes crossed and he tripped again.

Just then Pierre heard a loud snort. By the time he looked up, the moose was on its feet and bolting for cover. "Hey," he shouted. Pierre quickly shook a measure of powder into his gun, but by the time he rammed a ball home and fired, the moose was out of range.

After Red Loon untangled himself, they examined the

spot where the moose had fallen. Red Loon found a pale splash of blood and a pile of whitish hair. "He's shot in the guts." Red Loon shook his head.

When Red Loon went to reload his gun, he couldn't find his shot bag. They searched where he had fallen and back along the trail, but there was no sign of it. Since Pierre had mainly filled his pouch with grapeshot that morning, assuming they'd see more rabbits than deer, they were left with only a handful of musket balls.

"That's plenty if we shoot straight next time," Red Loon said, starting off on the trail of the wounded moose. The huge footprints and the spots of blood in the snow made the tracks impossible to miss.

Neither boy expected to see the moose again so soon, but after they'd walked only two hundred yards, it took off running through the thick brush. Red Loon took a hasty shot and missed. When Pierre fired, the animal went down. This time there were no cheers. Both boys reloaded as quickly as they could and started forward with their guns raised. When the animal leaped up again, they were ready. But this time the moose charged into a thick patch of willows, and both of their bullets were deflected.

Red Loon studied the place where the moose had fallen. "There's more blood, but I don't like how strongly he's running." Pierre could see that the moose had taken huge jumps through the willow swamp.

A short while later, Red Loon became more confident. "Look," he said, waving his mitt at the fresh sign, "he's walking now. It won't be long before he has to bed down."

A quarter of a mile further on, Red Loon whispered, "Get ready." He motioned toward a balsam thicket fifty yards ahead. Pierre checked his flint and raised his North West gun.

Red Loon stepped toward the trees. Pierre was expecting the moose to run out the east side of the thicket, so he sighted on an open patch of ground just beyond the trees. To his surprise, the moose charged out of the balsams right in front of them. Pierre swung his gun and fired too quickly. He heard his ball whiz over the moose's head and thwack into a tree.

Red Loon had a perfect shot, but when he pulled the trigger, there was a sickening click. By the time he blew his flint dry and recocked, the moose was running straight away. Red Loon missed clean.

"Now we're done," Red Loon said. "I should have been more careful with that last shot."

"At least you aimed," Pierre said. "I shot without even thinking."

Red Loon and Pierre studied the snow. The animal was bleeding more than ever, and it was clear that it would die.

"He's wolf bait now," Red Loon said, shaking his head. "That's a shame."

The boys turned to head home. Pierre felt terrible. His feet ached so badly that he was limping, and his heart was heavy. Not only would the children back at camp go without food, but because of their failure, a proud animal would also die an ignoble death and be left to feed the ravens and weasels.

What would Robinson Crusoe do in a situation like this? Pierre thought. "Wait a minute," he said, pulling his knife from his belt. "I've got an idea."

Red Loon frowned. "You're going to run him down and stab him?"

Pierre shook his head. "No." He smiled, sliding the tip of his knife into the screw that held the trigger guard of his North West gun. He hoped he wouldn't break the blade, which his old friend La Londe had tempered by hand. A few turns later Pierre had the heavy brass screw in his hand.

"Do you really think it will work?" Red Loon asked.

"Our cook says that in an emergency you can load these muskets with anything—stones, marbles, nails. So why not a screw?"

"It's worth a try," Red Loon agreed. "Besides, it shouldn't take much to bring him down now."

Pierre loaded his gun, and Red Loon led the way. After a half mile of careful stalking, Red Loon stopped to study the tracks. He looked ahead toward a rocky hillside that was covered with young spruce. "I'll bet he's right up there," he whispered.

Pierre nodded.

"I'll circle around the side of that hill," Red Loon continued. "When he scents me, he's bound to come right back down this trail."

161

As Red Loon worked his way quietly through the brush, Pierre positioned himself beside a big red pine. When he aimed, he would rest his gun against the side of the tree and take no chance on missing.

Just then he heard a loud crash. Instead of running south, the moose charged out of the trees directly toward Red Loon. Though Red Loon yelled and waved his arms, trying to turn the animal toward Pierre, it kept heading straight toward him.

Pierre tried to draw a bead on the animal, but he couldn't get a clear shot through the brush. He was ready to fire anyway when he remembered a hunting tip from his father.

Knowing that he had only seconds to act, Pierre whistled. His first try was weak, but his second whistle pierced the air with a clear, high note.

The moose stopped and swung his head in Pierre's direction. Pierre aimed for his front shoulder and squeezed. When the moose went down for good, Pierre and Red Loon let out a loud cheer.

Pierre snowshoed over to the fallen giant. As much as the camp needed meat, it still hurt Pierre to watch the life ebb out of the great creature. Though every hunt ended with the same green eyes—a "death glaze," his father had called it on that autumn day four years earlier when Pierre had shot his first deer—knowing it didn't blunt the pain.

For Pierre hunting was a mixture of joy and sadness. On one side was the need for food. On the other side was the right of wild creatures to run free. Pierre was confused whenever he tried to balance one against the other. As with so much of life, there was no simple answer—no clear right or wrong side.

"We did it," Pierre said, whispering without meaning to.

"You did it," Red Loon replied. His voice sounded as if his mind were far away.

"No, brother," Pierre insisted. "We did it. And to prove my point"—he paused with a wry smile and handed his knife to Red Loon—"the field dressing honors go to you."

"You shot it, you gut it, white man."

They both laughed softly, keeping their voices quiet out of respect.

Then Red Loon broke off a small aspen twig and placed it in the corner of the moose's mouth. Bowing silently, he whispered a prayer to honor the spirit of the animal. Next he touched his finger to a droplet of the moose's blood and marked Pierre's forehead with a bright streak of red. After he did the same to his own brow, he whispered, "From ashes to blood, the circle is once more perfect."

CHAPTER 20

Equinox

Pierre and Red Loon received a hero's welcome. It took a dozen men to pack the moose meat back to camp. The original plan was to divide the meat equally between the *voyageurs* and the Ojibwe, but when Pierre mentioned to Commander McHenry how short the tribe was of food, they left the bulk of it for the village.

When Rat's Liver protested, McHenry was insistent. "Just give us a few steaks," he said. "We've got a keg of pork fat left and lots of rice. Rice is really all we need, right, Louie?" He slapped Louie on the back.

Though Pierre could tell that Louie was hungry enough to devour a hunk of raw moose meat, Louie smiled, "That's right, Commander."

"Thank you, gentlemen," Rat's Liver said. "We will invite you all to a feast to celebrate our good fortune."

The moment Pierre stepped inside the bunkhouse, he was struck by an incredible weariness. His cheeks felt flushed, and his feet, which had been numb through the afternoon, suddenly began to ache. He sat down in front of the fireplace and struggled to untie the knotted laces of his moccasins.

"Did your feet get cold?" McHenry asked.

"A little," Pierre said as he struggled with the knots.

"How bad are they?"

"They're all tingly," Pierre admitted. "And that's what's so confusing. I hardly felt them all day."

"We'd better take a look," McHenry said, borrowing a sheath knife from Beloît and cutting away the still frozen laces.

As the commander pulled off Pierre's moccasins and socks, the *voyageurs* crowded near the fire to have a look. Pierre felt stupid with all the men gawking at his bare feet. "It's nothing," he insisted.

"We'll be the judge of that," the commander said.

Pierre looked at his feet. They were red and puffy, and his left big toe felt as if someone had driven a needle right through it.

"Looks like a touch of frostbite," Beloît declared over McHenry's shoulder.

"Aye," McHenry agreed. "Would one of you boys fetch a kettle of water?"

In a few minutes enough snow had been melted to half-fill a kettle with water. The men were anxious to help. "We got to take care of the only decent hunter in the whole crew," Bellegarde said.

When McHenry lowered Pierre's foot into the water, he had to clutch his hands together to keep from yelling. "That's hot!"

The commander looked worried. "It's barely lukewarm, son."

Two days later Pierre's foot was worse. Though the general swelling had gone down, his toe was puffed up to twice its normal size, and it was turning black.

When McHenry examined Pierre's foot that afternoon, he tried to distract Pierre with a story. "If you think it's cold around here, you should visit the Barrens sometime."

As McHenry probed at his toe, Pierre felt his whole body trembling. Since half the crew were watching, he tried not to flinch. "One day we cut down a dwarf spruce that was only eight feet high," McHenry continued, "but when we counted the growth rings on that little tree, we found it was three hundred years old. Further north, the trees stopped altogether. It's a vast arctic desert—totally flat with shallow muskeg lakes. What little moisture that does fall can't drain through the frost. The sun never sets in midsummer. Millions of ducks and geese nest up there, and there's an explosion of wildflowers the like of which you'll never see anywhere else on earth." For a moment Pierre forgot his pain as he pictured this rare flowering.

"The Indians from that country are called Chipeway-ans. They're a different tribe from the Chippewa. I was the first white man they'd ever seen." McHenry paused to grin. "They looked at me as if I'd just flown down from the moon. They stuck their fingers in my ears and nose and mouth. They laughed at my blond hair, which they said was as yellow as a pee-stained buffalo tail. They even pulled down my pants and giggled like little children when they found my whole body was the same pale color. When they finished, they declared me fit but 'weak-skinned.' "

Pierre laughed at the picture of the commander with his pants down. "So how's my foot?"

"To be honest, not good."

Pierre stared straight into McHenry's eyes. "How bad is it?"

"I'm sorry, Pierre. But before that poison spreads any further, we've got to take off your toe."

Pierre tried to fight back the tears. He thought of the thumb his father had lost the previous year in an accident cutting wood. Pierre could still close his eyes and see the doctor sewing the skin flap tight over the stub. He could see the bloody bandage his father bravely wore.

"Can't we wait just a little longer? Maybe it will—"

McHenry shook his head. "If it gets in your blood, you'll lose your foot or worse."

The pain in Pierre's toe was suddenly small compared to the cold clutch of fear in his stomach. "But what if it gets better?" he insisted.

"There's no time to waste, La Page." McHenry had assumed his commander's voice now. It was clear that he intended to proceed without delay.

McHenry turned to André. "Get some clean rags and—"

But before he could finish, Beloît interrupted. "Excuse me, sir," he began. Every head turned toward him. Pierre had never heard him say "excuse me" to anyone. "Little Cat fixed a boy in the village the other day who had an awful bad infection in his hand."

"We really don't have time to—"

"Please, sir," Pierre interrupted. "Can't we give it a try?"

McHenry was clearly impatient to get on with his surgery, but he consented.

When Beloît returned with Little Cat, she carried a steaming pot that smelled like pine needles. "What's that?" Pierre asked, wrinkling up his nose at the gooey yellow paste.

"The inner bark of tamarack, plus a few secret ingredients," she explained. Beloît winked at Little Cat and gave her a friendly pinch as she stirred the mixture. She giggled as usual.

Though her laughter didn't instill much confidence in Pierre, he was happy to delay the amputation. When Little Cat pulled out her knife, Pierre frowned.

"We need to open the wound," she explained with a smile, "to help the salve work."

Pierre wondered if he'd made the right choice. If he needed to be cut open, perhaps McHenry would offer a steadier hand? But Little Cat had already heated her knife blade over the fire and was reaching for his swollen foot.

McHenry offered a distraction. "But I never told you the strangest thing about those Chipewayans, Pierre. It was their medicine man. He had the usual spells and chants, but his specialty was stomach problems. For any intestinal complaints he had a cure-all that he used on everyone. To start with he'd puff out his cheeks and approach a certain, shall we say, southerly part of the patient's anatomy with a huge gust of wind."

"No," Pierre blurted out, ready to laugh but clenching his teeth tight instead as he felt the first cut of Little Cat's blade.

"I tell you," McHenry continued, "it was the most remarkable thing I've ever seen. And that fellow didn't care whether he was doctoring an old man or a pretty young gal; he treated everyone the same. He blew so hard that he'd make their eyes bulge, and the mess that followed was ghastly."

As Little Cat's knife sawed deeper and deeper into his flesh, Pierre felt as if he was going to throw up. Then everything went black.

CHAPTER 21

Sugar Bush

When Pierre awoke, Little Cat was standing over him, smiling. His foot throbbed with a burning, itchy feeling that made him want to scream. But when he looked down at the toe, its color was considerably better.

"What time is it?" he asked.

"Nearly time for breakfast, you lazy pup," Beloît piped up from behind. Pierre couldn't believe he'd slept through the night.

Pierre's foot ached for several days after Little Cat's treatment. She applied the tamarack paste twice daily, and the ugly infection gradually disappeared. McHenry was so impressed with Pierre's recovery that he gave Little Cat a present of a fine blanket and some ribbons.

* * *

"Hey, Pierre," Red Loon said, swinging open the door of the bunkhouse one morning in March. "The crows are back."

"So?" Pierre said. He swung his feet to the floor and yawned. It was just after dawn, and he was still half asleep. Why would the arrival of crows bring such excitement to Red Loon's eyes?

"That means the sap is running. My family is hiking up to the sugar bush, and Father says you can come with us if you like."

"When are you leaving?" Pierre asked.

"This morning," Red Loon said. He was already turning to head back to the village.

Pierre was still amazed at how quickly his Ojibwe friend made decisions. Red Loon lived for the moment and never fretted over detailed plans or preparations. Back home Pierre's parents discussed things forever. It didn't matter whether it was a small thing like buying a secondhand plow or a big thing like his sister Camille's marriage, they talked the matter to death. To make matters worse, when it was all over they often worried they'd made the wrong choice.

"Come if you can," Red Loon said as he turned toward the door.

"I'd have to ask the commander if . . . ," Pierre started to say.

171

But McHenry, who was already standing in the doorway, said, "We're still between seasons, Pierre. Take your holiday if you want. Just make sure you bring us some fresh maple candy."

"That's right." Beloît spoke from the long bench where he was repairing a snowshoe binding. "Some of us have got sweet tooths."

"There ain't nothing sweet about those rotten teeth of yours," La Petite called from the far corner. The rest of the men chuckled.

Beloît threw back his head and laughed, showing his tobacco-stained teeth. At least four or five were missing.

"It's my lips, not my teeth, that the *mesdemoiselles* kiss. A man only needs a tooth or two to tear his meat—the rest are all extras."

Pierre gagged at the thought of anyone kissing Beloît's deformed face. He was suddenly glad to be leaving, no matter how short the notice might be.

Within the hour he was trooping through the woods with Red Loon's extended family. Counting his aged grandfather and his young cousins, there were a dozen people. At first the frozen snow crust crunched loudly under their moccasins, but by midmorning the sun had softened the trail. The only sounds to disturb the silence of the forest were the occasional bark of a dog or the squeal of a baby.

"How far is it?" Pierre asked Red Loon.

"About five miles. In fact, it's just beyond that ridge where we took the moose."

"Why don't you just tap those big maples on that ridge above the post?"

"Another family camps in that stand. We have traveled to this same maple grove since my grandmother was a small child."

"Do you always leave this suddenly?"

"My grandfather decides." Red Loon smiled. "Once he hears that first crow, there's no holding him back. He knows the weather is changing. It takes frosty nights followed by sunny days to start the sap flowing."

For the next week Pierre lived with Red Loon's family in the sugar bush. The women and children tended the fires under the huge moosehide vats of sap that bubbled day and night, while the men went hunting. Returning each evening with game, they would feast on roast venison or partridge or rabbit, as the sweet scents of sugar and maple-wood smoke hung in the air.

Mornings were magical in the maple wood. After waking to a world of frosty silence, Pierre heard the first faraway plunk of a sap droplet landing in a birch bucket shortly after dawn. As the sun rose and the sap flow quickened, other drops hit other buckets across the forest. The symphony continued unabated until the cold arm of darkness came again and brought the pulse to rest.

Pierre could see why this was a special time for Red Loon's people. While the children played games, the old ones told stories about the sugar camps of years gone by.

There was a hint of winter at night, but the days were bright and warm.

"The voice of the crow was true in predicting a fine sap run," Pierre said one evening as they sat before the fire.

Red Loon nodded. With a smile he said, "The wild things can teach us much if we are willing to listen."

CHAPTER 22

Last Testament

It happened shortly after Pierre returned from the sugar bush. It was a perfect blue morning. Pierre was standing in the doorway of the bunkhouse, watching a distant smoke plume rise from the top of a wigwam. Beloît was outside, sitting on a log bench with his feet propped on a rum keg. Though he looked half asleep, the grizzled bowman suddenly sat up and stared down the bay.

"It's time for a change of diet, *hivernant*." Beloît punched La Petite in the shoulder to get his attention.

"What did you have in mind?" the big man replied.

"Look." Beloît waved his hand toward a flock of mallards that were landing in a open patch of water between the island and the shore. Though the main part of the lake was still locked in ice, the shoreline had begun to open in places.

La Petite scanned the horizon. "Ah." He grinned. "Roast duck."

"I can taste it already," Beloît said, striding into the bunkhouse and taking his North West gun down from the wall, where it had hung for the last month. "A finer fowling piece there never was than sweet Tillie." He kissed the brass dragon on the side plate of his rifle.

La Petite laughed and said, "If you treated your women as well as you treat that gun, you'd have married a dozen wives by now."

"I've had plenty of wives, but this little beauty has brought down more meat than a whole brigade of women could."

Chuckling, Beloît slung his powder horn and shot bag over his shoulder. He clenched his gun barrel like a walking stick and stepped toward the door, tapping the butt plate on the threshold.

Pierre thought a cannon had gone off. He ducked his head and covered his ears.

When he looked up, powder smoke was billowing out of the bunkhouse doorway. As the haze cleared, Pierre saw that though Beloît was still standing, the left side of his face was completely gone. Blood was splattered over the ceiling and floor.

As they helped Beloît to a bunk, Pierre was amazed that the bowman remained conscious. Though La Petite tried to quiet him, he insisted on talking. "It's lucky I shot myself in the left side, eh," he joked, lifting a trembling hand toward the bloody hole that had been his cheek. "That way I didn't mess up the pretty half of my face. *Je suis l'homme.*"

"I'll get help," Pierre said, turning toward the door.

"No," Beloît groaned.

When Pierre stopped, Beloît's voice dropped to a whisper. "Come here, pup." He chuckled hoarsely. "There's not much time." Pierre stepped toward the bunk.

Though Beloît's breathing was labored and he was clearly in excruciating pain, he continued. "Since I got no kin, I want to leave you my year's salary."

"But why me?" Pierre stared.

"Apply the money to your schooling. Any of these rascals"—he waved his hand toward the men who were crowding through the door—"would waste it on whiskey and wenches. You got a chance to become someone."

Pierre was about to say more when the bowman motioned toward La Petite.

La Petite knelt to towel away the blood that was trickling down Beloît's neck, but Beloît brushed his hand aside. "I sure spoiled our duck hunt, didn't I?"

"Don't—"

"You see they bury me proper," Beloît cut in.

"You're not going to die."

"Spare me the lies." Beloît coughed. "I'm dead already." The big steersman leaned close to hear his raspy voice. Pierre missed the next few sentences, but suddenly Beloît spoke loudly enough for the whole room to hear. "When it's over, I want you to throw my carcass in a hole up in those red pines. Don't waste no burying clothes on me neither. I want to go out of this world the same way I came in—naked and ugly as sin." Beloît started to chuckle, but he coughed and gagged instead. The blanket beneath his head was soaked with blood.

By the time Beloît caught his breath, Little Cat had arrived with some bandages. But when she bent down to wrap the blue gingham across his face, he shook his head. "Save it for a kerchief," he whispered.

Little Cat sobbed softly as La Petite urged, "Just rest now," but Beloît continued.

"And I'll have no Bible thumping. If there's any preaching, I'll haunt every pipe stop and portage from here to Montréal." He grinned.

"When it's all done"—he gulped a shallow breath— "don't be breaking up a good paddle to make a cross. Plant me a tree."

Beloît fell into a fitful sleep. Throughout the day, Little Cat and Clear Sky took turns holding a cool rag to his feverish head and waiting. Little Cat sobbed the whole time.

"Hush, woman," Beloît mumbled, but there was no stopping her tears.

As Pierre tried to comfort Little Cat, he thought how strange it was for him to feel sorry for this man who had ridiculed him for two years. Beloît's sudden generosity made Pierre wonder if he'd been hiding a gentler side all along.

However, if there was any real goodness in the bow-man, he didn't let a hint of it show during his final moments on earth. Just when Beloît was struggling to draw in his last ragged breath, he opened one eye. Pierre jerked back from the sudden black sneer.

As weak as Beloît was, there was no mistaking his final words. "Stoke up the fire," he rasped. "I'm going straight to the devil."

Turning to Little Cat, he whispered, "Don't grieve, honey pot. You'll find yourself another fellow. You shouldn't never have to be lonesome."

Then, nodding toward the men who were gathered near the door, he rasped, "Keep your powder dry, boys."

Pierre waited for Beloît to take another gulp of air. Without realizing it, Pierre held his own breath too. His head was light. His heart pounded until he felt as if his temples were about to explode. Just then he read the cold, unfocused stare in Beloît's eyes. It was done.

Little Cat let out a high-pitched wail and threw herself onto Beloît's chest.

Pierre stepped outside and drew a deep breath. The twilight was heavy with the scent of dew. McHenry's "Sorry, lad," sounded far away, and Pierre barely felt the gentle pat of Rat's Liver's hand on his shoulder. Pierre walked numbly to the lake. He was a stranger, standing outside himself, even as he watched the dying light above Daisy Island turn the horizon to pale fire.

Pierre had often wished Beloît dead, but now that it had happened, he felt guilty. No one—not La Londe, not Kennewah, not even Beloît—deserved to be struck down in his prime. Death should be only for the old.

Pierre walked east along the beach, never stopping until he reached the edge of a cedar grove. He paused and looked up at a huge tree. Though its dark, spiraled trunk was already lost in shadow, the upper branches glowed with green and golden light. Pierre couldn't help smiling when he recalled how often he'd come to this place to escape Beloît's mad cackling. But now that the fool was dead, Pierre knew he would miss him.

They dug a grave as Beloît had asked on the hill above the post, and they buried their bowman the next morning. Beloît's canoe mates carried his body up to the pine grove, followed by most of the Ojibwe band and Marie Antoinette, who appeared as if on schedule. The little bear had just crawled out of her den that week, and she wandered back and forth among the mourners, whining softly as she had on the day Beloît rescued her.

The grave was at the base of a huge red pine. Smelling of sweet loam, it reminded Pierre of the flower beds his mother would be planting back in Lachine about now. When they pulled the blanket off Beloît and lowered him into the grave, Pierre was stunned by the paleness of the bowman's skin. His naked body looked blindingly white against the dark soil. His chest was scarred from a knife fight, and his left shoulder was marked with the imprint of a large pair of teeth. Pierre wondered if the tooth marks were from the same man who'd bitten off half of Beloît's nose.

Little Cat, who had been wailing plaintively through most of the night, had painted Beloît's cheeks with two brown circles and drawn a finger-wide strip of vermilion through them. "The paint is to make him ready for the ghost dance in the northern sky," Red Loon whispered. "The food is to keep him from going hungry on his four days' journey to the hereafter."

With her own cheeks blackened to show her grief, Little Cat knelt at the edge of the grave and lowered a kettle of rice, a knife, and a tobacco pouch to Beloît's side. When she unsheathed a second knife, Pierre feared that she intended to do herself harm. But before he could step forward, Red Loon touched his arm. "It is the proper thing to do," he whispered.

Pierre was relieved when she only sawed off her hair and dropped it into the grave. The coarse sound of the blade hacking off handfuls of her long, silky hair, accompanied as it was by the wailing of Little Cat and her family, sent chills up Pierre's spine. The bear nosed Little Cat's arm gently as she sobbed.

When Commander McHenry stepped forward, Bible in hand, La Petite said, "I'm sorry, sir."

McHenry began, "But surely someone should—"

"I gave him my word."

Pierre thought back to the poetic verse Commander

John McKay had read the previous summer over Pierre's drowned comrade, La Londe: "Man that is born of a woman is of few days, and full of trouble. He cometh forth like a flower, and is cut down: he fleeth also as a shadow, and continueth not." At first Pierre regretted there would be no such recitation today. But when he searched his mind for a poem or a Bible verse that Beloît might like, he drew a blank. Perhaps silence was better than a sea chant or a tavern song?

"It don't seem right," Louie mumbled, "to bury a fellow without so much as a single prayer."

La Petite then turned to Pierre. "He asked you to throw in the first clod of dirt."

"What?" Pierre frowned.

"He said, 'Give that kid a fistful of dirt and let him dump it right on my face. Lord knows I deserve it after all the ribbing I gave him.'"

Numbly Pierre knelt and picked up a handful of damp earth. It smelled of pine needles and April wind. Pierre crumbled the black soil between his fingers and let it fall gently onto the pale man's chest. Pierre trembled as he stared at the cold body. It seemed as if he'd met this laughing fool only yesterday at the fur depot back in Lachine. And wasn't it only a moment ago that Beloît had been sitting on a rum keg in the sun?

A single misstep and a powder flash later, he had come to this. It was hard for Pierre to find any meaning or purpose in such random happenings. He wondered: Is each day given to us as a gift to relish, or is life only a cruel trick waiting for the ancient woodland trickster Winibojo to show his hand?

The sound of yesterday's gunshot was still echoing in Pierre's head as he held his empty hand over the grave and watched the shadows of the pines play across Beloît's face.

After they had filled in the hole, La Petite took out a paddle, sharpened on the handle end. Using the flat side of a hatchet, he drove it into the ground at the head of the grave. On the blade he'd carved the initials *JBB*.

"He didn't want any crosses," La Petite explained, "but I figured we needed something to mark this little tree here." He knelt then, scooped out a handful of dirt, and planted a white pine seedling. "Maybe one day this will grow up to be a lob pine, tall enough to mark a journey by."

As La Petite finished, a little Ojibwe boy stepped forward and placed a piece of maple candy beside the seedling. La Petite said, "Thank you, son," then turned to the whole group. "The one thing Beloît did ask was that you all meet together back at the trading post, so I could make an announcement."

Pierre noticed strange expressions on the men as they made their way back down the hill. Some looked as if they'd been told half a joke and were waiting for the rest. A few whispered about how strange it felt to bury a man that way. Others just shook their heads.

A short while later, the *voyageurs* and Ojibwe gathered outside the post to listen to La Petite. "Whether you liked

Beloît or not," La Petite began, "we can all agree that he never pretended to be something he wasn't." Several heads nodded.

"I know we've barely had time to finish our breakfast, and we've been to a burying and all, but Beloît wanted us to do one last thing. Since he was a heap more partial to celebrating than preaching, he asked if you gentlemen would empty a rum keg."

The men were stunned. They had expected a long-winded eulogy. For a moment no one moved. Augustine finally grinned when he realized he'd been ordered to have a party. Throwing his hat into the air along with a half dozen other men, he shouted, "To the memory of Jean-Baptiste Beloît."

CHAPTER 23

Grand Portage Bound

As soon as Vermilion was free of ice, the brigade headed back to the Crane Lake post to reunite with the crewmen who'd wintered up on Quetico Lake. Along with the bundled furs, Pierre's canoe carried one more bit of freight: McHenry's young wife, Clear Sky. Though some of the men questioned the wisdom of bringing a native wife back east, McHenry was committed to doing so. "I've wandered enough years in the wilderness," he said. "It's time for me to settle down with this good woman and try my hand at honest work."

The day before the brigade left, Pierre and Louie stopped by the village and invited Red Loon to help them with a project.

"How would you like to help us with a little tree climbing?" Pierre asked.

Red Loon frowned. "What sort of tree did you have in mind?"

"We were thinking of a certain prominent pine that stands just up the ridge," Louie said.

"You know the one." Pierre got serious. "It stands above Beloît's grave. We got to thinking about what La Petite said at the funeral when he planted that little seedling."

"About it growing into a lob pine?" Red Loon recalled.

"That's right," Pierre said. "We thought it might be fun to limb that tree right up to the crown."

Red Loon was suddenly excited. "I've seen those big lob pines that mark the main canoe routes up on La Croix."

"Don't you think it's about time Lake Vermilion had its own little marker?" Louie asked.

"Let me get my hatchet," Red Loon said.

Two hours later the boys were scratched and covered with sap, but they were satisfied. With the help of a rope, they'd scaled the giant pine and lopped off every limb all the way up to the great crown on top.

They took a canoe from the village and paddled out into Big Bay. The huge pine, bare and tall, projected a full twenty-five feet above the tree line. "You'll be able to see that thing from five miles away," Louie said in awe.

Red Loon and Pierre nodded and smiled in agreement.

Suddenly Red Loon frowned. "Didn't Beloît say he only wanted a little sapling for a grave marker?"

"That's right." Louie grinned.

"Besides," Pierre added, "when was the last time Beloît ever followed directions?" The boys had a good laugh as they paddled back to the village.

They kept the tree a secret until the day of their departure. As the *voyageurs* were loading the last of the fur bales into their canoes, Rat's Liver and Red Loon walked down to the shore to say goodbye.

With a grin Red Loon handed Pierre a canoe paddle.

"Abwi." Pierre smiled, remembering the Ojibwe name for a full-sized paddle.

Red Loon nodded. "My uncle made it specially for you. He said, 'Pierre must not return home with a woman's paddle.' "

"Give your uncle my thanks," Pierre said, reaching into his pack and pulling out a red cap. "To keep you warm."

"I will think of you when the snows are deep," Red Loon said.

"One day I will return to Vermilion," Pierre said, embracing his friend one last time.

Rat's Liver shook McHenry's hand and turned to Pierre. Touching the rawhide cord around Pierre's neck, the chief said, "Remember your true name, White Hawk.

No matter how far you travel, the power of this place will go with you, and your *manitou* will protect you all the days of your life."

"Time to voyage, gentlemen," McHenry said, striding toward the waiting canoes.

When the men had pulled clear of the island and headed out into open water, La Petite turned to have one last look at the fort.

"What the—" the big man began.

Other heads turned. "Would you look at that?" André said. "It's a lob pine. Who on earth ever would have . . . ?"

By then the boys were laughing. As the rest of the crew realized what they'd done, they all began laughing too.

"Ol' Beloît's got himself the biggest blessed grave marker this side of—" André was stumped, trying to find the proper word.

"Let's be honest, gentlemen," McHenry said. "Shall we say the biggest marker this side of Hades?"

With that they all had one last chuckle before they struck off for the north shore of Vermilion.

When McHenry's brigade arrived at Crane Lake, the first man to greet them was Maurice Blondeau, from the brigade that had wintered on Quetico. After shaking hands all around, Blondeau asked, "So where is that idiot Beloît?"

When McHenry gave him the news, Blondeau's first

reaction was disbelief. The Quetico group realized it was not a joke, and everyone stood in awkward silence for a long time.

Pierre could understand their shock; Beloît had seemed indestructible. McHenry summed it up. "I would have wagered a year's pay that Beloît would have lived long enough to wear out many rocking chairs in his retirement."

After a quieter than normal bragging session that evening, the *voyageurs* retired early. Waking well before dawn, they loaded their pelts into the four North canoes and set off on the two-hundred-mile paddle to Grand Portage. Though the canoes were heavily laden, favorable winds helped the crew make good time. A steady breeze blew out of the west, allowing the men to put up makeshift sails, and they crossed the big water of Lac la Croix, Crooked, and Basswood in half the time it normally took.

When they reached Saganaga four days later, Pierre was shocked to see that the south shore was still black from the previous summer's fire. "They say the blaze smoldered until the first snows," La Petite remarked as he surveyed the destruction.

In the low country fresh shoots of ferns and wild grasses were brightening the ground, but the rocky ridges remained black and barren. The charred snags stood as grim reminders of the fire. Though the sun was bright and warm, the dead branches recalled a bitter winter day.

The *voyageurs* paddled the length of Saganaga in rare

silence, staring at the dead land. Pierre winced as they paddled past their old campsite. He remembered the yellow wind, the roaring fire, and the little squirrel that leaped flaming into the lake. He would never forget its death shriek.

At the far end of Saganaga, just as the brigade was getting ready to portage into the Granite River, a young bear appeared at the edge of the water. Instead of running into the underbrush as Pierre expected, it stared curiously at the approaching canoes. The crew put down their paddles, and Maurice Blondeau pulled out a North West gun. Don't shoot, Pierre was ready to yell, but La Petite reached out with his long steersman's paddle and tipped the gun barrel down.

"What in the blazes do you think you're—" Maurice stopped when he saw that every man in La Petite's canoe was staring silently at him.

The little bear stood his ground. Even as the canoes drifted closer, the bear tipped his head and studied the men intently.

Amblé Le Clair was the first to take off his cap, and in a moment, every man who had wintered on Vermilion followed suit. The men from the Quetico group stared at this odd salute. Pierre smiled. He was impressed that the brigade would pass up a chance for roast bear to honor the memory of Jean Beloît.

Only when the bow of La Petite's canoe touched the shore did the bear finally move. Even then he sauntered away slowly, turning twice to look at the men before he disappeared. "What a brave little fellow," Pierre whispered.

When Maurice asked, "What on earth is going on?" the men only smiled.

Pierre knew they would tell the whole story later that evening. He could see the canoemen standing by the fire and lifting their cups to toast Beloît. There would be many bold tales to tell, but for now it was good to listen to the silence of the forest.

Pronunciation Guide for French Names and Other Words

André Bellegarde   (On-DRAY Bell-GARD)

Jean Beloît   (ZHON Buh-LWA)

Maurice Blondeau   (Mo-REECE Blon-DO)

Jacques Charbonneau   (ZHAK Shar-bo-NO)

Augustine Delacroix   (O-goos-TEEN Duh-la-KRWAH)

Pierre La Page   (Pee-AIR La PAHZH)

Joseph La Petite   (Zho-SEF La Pe-TEET)

Amblé Le Clair   (Ahm-BLAY Luh CLARE)

à la façon du pays   (a la fa-SON doo pa-YEE)

bonjour   (bon-ZHURE)

capote   (ca-POTE)

chanson   (chahn-SOHN)

hivernant   (ee-ver-NAN)

hommes du nord   (OM doo NOR)

Je suis l'homme   (zhu swee LOM)

La belle Lisette, chantait l'autre   (La BELL Lee-ZET, shan-TAY LOE-treh)

madame   (mah-DAM)

mademoiselle   (mad-mwa-ZELLE)

marche   (march)

mesdemoiselles   (may-duh-mwa-ZELL)

monsieur   (muh-see-YUR)

sacré bleu   (SACK-ray-BLUH)

sacré chien mort   (SACK-ray she-AHN MOR)

Vive Napoléon   (VEEV na-po-le-ON)

voyageur   (voy a-ZHUR)

Pronunciation Guide for Objibwe Names and Other Words

Anishinaabe   (a-NI-shi-NAA-bay)

Gageanakwad   (Ga-GAY-a-NA-KWAD)

Gasigens   (GAA-zhi-gayns)

Kennewah   (Key-NA-wah)

Mide Manido   (mi-DAY Ma-ni-DO)

Mukwa   (Ma-KWA)

Odinigun   (O-DIN-i-GUN)

Ojibwe   (O-JI-bway)

Onabinigizis   (O-NAA-bi-ni-GEE-zis)

Wawa'ckeci nonda' gotcigun   (waa-waa-SHKAY-shi noon-DA go-zi-gun)

Winibojo   (WI-na-BOO-zhoo)

abwi   (a-BWI)

ikweabwi   (i-KWAY-a-BWI)

manitou   (ma-ni-DOO)

manomin   (ma-NO-min)

me-e-mengwe   (may-may-NGWAH)

midewin   (mi-DAY-win)

nibowin   (ni-BO-win)

wattape   (wah-TAH-pay)